God Atlas Media
www.GodAtlas.com
office@GodAtlas.com
1.800.519.4770

God Atlas Media
8194 W. Deer Valley Rd. Suite 106
Peoria, Arizona 85382

www.TerranceAdam.com

Text copyright © 2020 by Terrance Froysland
Cover design by Lance Buckley
Book design by Tobi Carter

ISBN 978-1-7358093-0-4 (hardcover)
ISBN 978-1-7358093-1-1 (paperback)
ISBN 978-1-7358093-2-8 (e-book)

THE
POKER
PLAYER
AND THE
PREACHER

TERRANCE ADAM

*For the Lost, Fence Walkers and
Ninety Percenters.*

T. Adam

CONTENTS

PROLOGUE

COVINGTON, ALABAMA – SEPTEMBER 2000

Adam Foster stood stone still in the middle of twelve hundred people, all there to see "The Preacher," the man who had impacted so many in such a short period of time. They also came to support Annabelle Perkins, a semi-successful gospel singer who'd become a top Christian television and radio personality. Her vision to build a Christian community center that would serve the families of her hometown, had come to fruition, commencing with a four-day launch.

The lights flickered in the rear of the auditorium, and with the opening of each door, more people searched for space to stand. The building wasn't finished, so the support beams and floors remained unfinished concrete. It may have been September outside, but it felt like summer in the auditorium, with everyone packed in tight, causing the temperature to increase by the minute. The Preacher was the last speaker—the one everyone came to see—and the excitement in the air was palpable. The room went dark, then the band erupted into song and drove the energy higher as the crowd sang along.

Jacob O'Shea, otherwise known as "The Preacher," walked onto the stage to almost deafening cheers. Standing next to the lead singer, with his arms in the air, he encouraged everyone to sing along. The man was genuine, his calling undeniable. He used his brilliant mind to communicate the most difficult concepts of the Bible to anyone willing to listen. His love of theology was contagious, and those who heard him preach the Word of God seemed to always want more.

His greatest gift was understanding his audience, reaching them where they were in their faith walk. It didn't matter if someone was studying for a doctorate in theology or had just graduated eighth grade, The Preacher's message would reach them if they had an ear to hear. He preached with the skill of a surgeon, and when necessary with the blunt force of a sledgehammer—telling it like it was, making no excuses in his quest to preach the truth.

The message flowed through him, and the audience connected with his genuine passion for the things of God. He brought those listening clear understanding, answering many of the most difficult questions that people of all levels of faith had a hard time asking— the ones that people mistook as questioning God rather than seeking enlightenment or clarity.

The Preacher was the reason Adam stood waiting, hoping many of the questions he asked would be answered at least in part. He wasn't naïve or expecting a miracle, but was praying that he would receive insight and guidance for his pursuit of understanding. He'd driven two thousand miles to hear this man deliver a message in person. Two things he knew for certain: it was a blessing to have the opportunity, and he would be leaving with as many tapes as a hundred and twenty dollars could buy.

The lead singer gave an introduction and handed over the mic. Standing just under six foot, The Preacher looked to be a solid two hundred twenty-five pounds, and was dressed in a traditional black suit and shirt with a white collar. He had an olive complexion and dark wiry hair cut short, and the lines of his well-trimmed beard seemed perfectly symmetrical. At only thirty-five years old, he had risen to the elite of academia but never lost touch with the basic principles found in the words of Jesus.

He thanked everyone for coming to hear him speak, as well as Mrs. Perkins, the organizers, and other guests for taking the time to support the tremendous vision that was now Covington Christian Community Center, then asked everyone to bow their heads and prayed that God, above all else, would be the audience's focus for the evening. The Preacher's goal was for everyone to leave the event wanting to know God more.

Adam raised his head when the crowd said, "Amen." The Preacher came alive, launching into an explanation of creation in relation to time, space, and motion with such simplicity that a fifth grader could have grasped the concept. He engaged the audience, firing off answers to questions they all had but were afraid to ask. The examples he provided brought clarity to his answers, allowing the listener to come full circle in every scenario.

He flowed through the sermon, building on concepts and allowing the audience to make connections. He asked, "How can God move? If God moved, then wherever God moved from would cease to exist. Therefore, the proper statement would be that we moved in God, for God is in all things at all times at the same time."

"He is the same yesterday, today, and tomorrow," The Preacher continued. "God doesn't change. He is absolute truth, his Word is in all of us. Truth rests in the Holy Spirit, the truth of God lives inside you. When God spoke the universe into existence, it was with words. His words hold the power of creation."

So much knowledge was delivered within his two-hour sermon that when he finished his closing prayer, no one moved. Only after several minutes of near silence did people head toward the exits, and they went slowly, seemingly lost in thought as they processed what they had heard.

Adam waited for most of the audience to leave before knocking on the door that led to the backstage area. He wasn't sure what led him to try, but he didn't want to leave without meeting the man who had helped put his mind at peace.

The door opened, and The Preacher stood in front of him.

In a moment of pure truth, Adam simply thanked him and asked to shake his hand.

He stuck out his hand with a smile. "It would be an honor to shake the hand of a young man seeking a stronger relationship with his creator. Remember we are the same—two people living entirely different lives yet ultimately seeking the same goal: to fulfill God's purpose for our life. Have a safe trip home, my friend."

Adam watched as the door closed. Hopefully, one day they would meet again.

CHAPTER 1

FLORIDA, 2019

The ocean breeze flooded Adam's car as he drove down the A1A toward St. Augustine. He refused to roll up the windows, welcoming the cool air and intermittent sprinkle of rain. It was worth it to take in the smell of salt air and hear the noise of the ocean waves crashing in. When no cars were oncoming, he carefully glanced out at the beach. The intracoastal waterway could be seen on the other side of the A1A, but he preferred to look at the ocean. On this part of coast especially, houses were sparse, allowing a clear view of the Atlantic that stretched as far as the eye could see. Peacefulness radiated from the cloudy sky that cast down shadows of light in shades of gray across the horizon.

Adam was looking for escape and hoped to find it in the beautiful natural distractions that surrounded him. The swaying of the elephant grass across the dunes, the seagulls that circled and randomly dove for fish, and the sound of wind whipping around him. Normally he could block the past from his mind, but today the memories flooded his consciousness. There was no rest between the flashbacks.

Once a memory was disposed of, another took its place. The closer he got to St. Augustine, the worse it became, but he wasn't turning the car around.

This was his last night in Jacksonville. Tomorrow he would play in the tournament final. After that, straight to the airport and then back to Arizona. He was looking forward to heading home. It was time to take a break from the road. At first, he never considered making the hour drive down the coast to St. Augustine, or at least that's what he told himself. The truth was the idea had been hiding in his thoughts since he chose to compete in the 5k invitational poker tournament in Jacksonville. He might have blown the trip off and headed back to the hotel for dinner and sleep if it wasn't for the onslaught of unwelcomed memories. He'd hoped the drive would help, and even though it wasn't working, he knew sitting in the hotel alone with his thoughts would have been far worse.

Adam pulled into the town parking lot not far from Flagler College, about a five-minute stroll through the park to the A1 Ale House. He settled into a table by the window, enjoying the view of the Bridge Alliance and the European feel of the nation's oldest city. Soon the ordered artichoke and blue crab dip along with a tall Yuengling arrived. Not his typical Guinness, but the beer was from the oldest brewery in the United States and it felt right in the moment.

As he ate, he glanced back and forth between his phone and the people walking past the window. The memories wouldn't stop coming, as though every mistake he'd made decided to haunt him at once. He couldn't stop the barrage of regret, frustration, sadness, disgust, anger, and shame.

After paying the bill, Adam walked a few blocks, taking in the sound of bands playing in the restaurants lining the street. On his way back to the rental car, he made the decision to drive by his parents' house. There was no way he'd stop, but he hoped it would settle his mind enough to push the mistakes of the past back into the dark recesses of his memory. He hadn't spoken to any of his family for over fifteen years. Simply driving by seemed childish, but that was as close as he was willing to get.

Another two miles down the coast, Adam turned onto George Street and took a left into the gated subdivision. He continued past the small lake at the center of the development and slowly turned onto Tash Avenue. People stood in his parents' front yard by the driveway, and when he got closer, he recognized his parents, two brothers, and their wives and children. They looked to be saying their goodbyes after an evening spent together, with his parents waving as the families got into their vehicles. A special occasion, or just dinner with family after a day at the beach?

Adam rolled past the house, watching his parents take the stone walkway to the front door. His father glanced back at the car, then opened the door for his mother. They looked well. Time had been good to them.

The ride back to the hotel was filled with a sense of loss coupled with the what-ifs that life had created. It was an odd feeling, like a story that ended to soon and left the reader wanting more. For a moment he smiled, thinking of all the good memories, but they were quickly chased off by the bad ones.

His mind was spiraling again by the time he reached the hotel. Anxiety overwhelmed him, sending sweat down his back. All he wanted was a break, but the memories refused to give him a moment's rest.

He grabbed two bottles of water from the table in the entryway to his suite, then went inside and sat down in the chair by the window. Outside, lanterns illuminated the walkways. He couldn't remember the last time he'd felt so overwhelmed. He needed to silence his thoughts, but Irish whiskey wasn't an option with the final table starting in less than twelve hours.

Adam got up, opened the nightstand drawer, and pulled out the book he hadn't opened in years. He climbed onto the bed, stretched his legs out with the Bible resting on his lap, and turned to Philippians. "Do not be anxious about anything, but in every situation, by prayer and petition, with thanksgiving present your requests to God."

He recited the words over and over, blocking out all other thoughts. The Scripture occupied his mind like a spiritual forcefield. Nothing could penetrate it.

Adam woke to the sound of the alarm on his phone, still dressed and lying on top of the covers. The Bible lay next to him on the bed. He showered, dressed, and packed before heading to the hotel restaurant for breakfast. The plan was to leave directly from the casino, so he'd scheduled his flight assuming that he would win and be the last to leave. It was much easier to catch an earlier flight than to call during the tournament hoping for a later flight. His mind was clear and free, so he was careful not to think about the previous day's events. His plan was simple: work to win the tournament, catch his flight home, and never look back.

———

Third place was taken by a local amateur who earned his way into the annual 5k invitational through a satellite tournament three weeks prior. His pride in the accomplishment was evident in the huge smile on his face as he thanked the audience for their support, hugged his wife, and followed the tournament officials to collect his $234,000 prize. Not a bad payday for a produce manager from the local Publix grocery store.

That was the beauty of poker—especially tournament poker—the allure that brought so many amateurs to the tables. It was the chance to win, and unlike the lottery or games of pure chance, it required strategy, patience, endurance, and the ability to problem solve quickly under pressure. Ultimately, only three decisions could be made—fold, call, or raise—making the game appear simplistic when in truth it was tremendously complex.

That left two at the final table heads-up, with the winner taking home $987,000 and the runner-up $525,000. The money was of course important to both men, but they had history, so winning and outplaying the other was the goal. Having gone heads-up on several occasions, they and their rivalry were legendary in the poker world.

This had begun over ten years ago during their first heads-up match, when they were just cutting their teeth. That match was affectionately known as "The Hand," and highlights were still shown regularly on the poker networks and online. People dissected, argued, and shared how they would have played it differently given the opportunity. Since then, these two players had battled on tables all over the world. They were polar opposites, both brilliant at the game, and it was no secret there was no love lost between them.

Many of the professional players who lost during the four-day tournament—the locals and amateurs—stuck around to play cash games. They also kept their eyes out to see if it would come down to these two players. So many stories had been told over the years that the truth and the tales became blurred along the way.

Scheduled to play heads-up at the Everest Hotel and Casino on the tenth anniversary of The Hand, in six weeks, spectators were hoping for a preview. The odds had been posted months ago in sportsbooks from Macau to Sydney, and this was a prelude to the main event. The outcome could result in bookmakers changing the odds over the course of the coming weeks.

Alan Dushku, known as "The Assassin," had gotten his nickname by having an unsettling ability to read his opponent and attack with perfect timing. His style of play was already aggressive, but when he got in his opponent's head, his reads were uncanny—often causing so much confusion between his bluffs and legitimate hands that opponents would become frustrated and lose focus.

Alan was there to collect their chips and send them home trying to figure out where things went wrong. Born in the former Yugoslavia, his parents escaped the destruction caused by the fall of the Soviet Union, initially landing in New York. After five years there, they moved their family to Tucson, Arizona. Alan's parents were hard workers who instilled the value of opportunity in their young son.

His passion from a young age was mathematics, and he would use this drive and his natural abilities in mathematics to graduate with a full academic scholarship to the University of Arizona, where he studied theoretical physics and applied mathematics. In graduate school he was introduced to poker, and within a month he had walked away from academia to chase the money.

It didn't take Alan long to be noticed, and a year later he found himself heads-up at the Everest, playing what would be known as The Hand. No one was prepared for the impact that match would have over the next ten years. He used his platform to create multiple streams of income, making him the richest "on-paper" poker player in the world. He utilized all social media platforms, giving a controlled window into his extravagant lifestyle, created a clothing line, endorsed numerous products, and had a lucrative contract for personal appearances.

A savvy businessman, it was his proposal to the management of the Everest that sold them on the ten-year anniversary rematch of The Hand. He also convinced them to put up $5 million in addition to the $30 million each player would bring to the table. He needed Everest to back the event, and he needed the casino to convince Adam "The Sleeper" Foster to participate, which was no small task. What it took to get Adam to sign on was never disclosed, and Alan didn't care. This was a payday for him, a chance to cement his legacy.

Adam Foster was a bit of an enigma. Not much was known about him, and he declined to make many comments. In his twenty-year career, he had granted a total of three interviews, and those three journalists later leaked that the questions were provided to Adam in advance for his approval. The Sleeper had no social media presence of his own, making him the exact opposite of The Assassin. Adam avoided the spotlight, and when he played, he never announced his arrival or departure. People never knew when or if he would partici-pate in a tournament or cash game.

What was known about him were the basics that could be found easily with a simple internet search. He had a wife, Lizzy, and two kids, Theodore and Lilly. They had houses in Arizona and New Orleans. His net worth varied by source, from $75 million to $150 million, and any number was a guess since no one knew for sure. Even the stories that moved through the poker rooms had no consistency, so no one bothered to listen anymore. The line between fact and fiction had been blurred so long ago that the truth existed somewhere in the middle. In a tight-knit community of the top fifty players, he had a few acquaintances but no friends. No one knew him well or spent time with him in the travel and marathon games that constituted most of their lives. He moved among them like a ghost.

Even where he got the nickname "The Sleeper" was an argument, whether it was his style of play, unpredictability, or near-motionless presence at the tables that made many players uncomfortable. Adam would sit seemingly asleep, stone still, appearing completely detached from the game. Sometimes for hours he would stare at nothing, responding to no one, his only movement coming from checking his cards. Then in a flash of brilliance he would engage. Amid the randomness of his play between the periods of statuesque resolve coupled with an unwillingness to even acknowledge conversation, his stack of chips would grow. This caused a variety of emotional reactions from other players, ranging from intense anger to pure hatred. Adam didn't care. Any emotion in the game of poker caused players to make mistakes, take it personal, and ultimately walk away as he scooped up the remnants of their last-ditch effort to win.

One amateur poker player who had a strong presence on social media with the handle "Pokerfish" was driven to make money and fuel his celebrity. He even put together a video of every tournament Adam won and added his reaction, making silly comments poking fun at the poker star. Amid a barrage of profanity and offensive comments, he pointed out how Adam never so much as cracked a smile, even when they presented him with the check.

Pokerfish's real name was Donald Lebowitz, and he went too far and blindly included Adam's wife in his unprovoked attacks. When

Adam's attorneys, led by Ramos Copperwood, a former senator from Louisiana, were finished with Mr. Lebowitz, he lost his house, the restaurant that had been in his family for three generations, his marriage, and—in a drunken state one cold December night—his life. When he threw himself off the Commodore Barry Bridge not far from his hometown of Wilmington, Delaware. The story was a footnote in the local papers and not even picked up by regional news, but in the poker community it spread like wildfire. Different reactions abounded, but one constant theme that cemented Adam's legend was that on the tables, as in life, he was void of emotion, coldhearted and ruthless.

Alan wore a gray Brioni suit, a crisp white collared shirt, and his trademark Versace sunglasses that hid deep-blue eyes. He was average size, with pale skin and shaggy brown hair. Sitting across the table, with a stack of just over $1.5 million separating them, was Adam, dressed in his customary hooded sweatshirt, jeans, and Nike Air Force Ones. He had an athletic build, and the only luxury item he ever wore was a Paul Newman Rolex Daytona. Except to people who knew watches, its subdued style and stainless-steel construction belied that it was incredibly rare and valuable. It was worth ten times more than the flashy diamond-encrusted Breitling Alan wore, which in a way was symbolic of their differences.

The gallery was packed, with standing room only as the television announcers hyped up the showdown. The universal announcement known to all players erupted from the speakers: "Cards in the air!"

Alan's starting chip count of $14 million was just five percent higher than Adam's $13.3 million, giving both players nearly equal chips to start. The match was underway, cards sliding, each player with a distinct handling of their cards. Alan lifted the corner of each card as he received it, while Adam cupped his hands, peeking at them once he had both. Neither way was correct—it was just their unique style, always the same a habit adopted and rooted in repetition.

The crowd was quiet, making the atmosphere feel more like The Masters in Augusta rather than a high-stakes showdown within the walls of a Jacksonville card room. The Assassin glanced first at the ace of clubs and then a king of clubs—Big Slick, the fifth-best starting hand in poker. In heads-up poker, more than likely an ace and king would result in Alan going all in.

Alan was the first to act, raising $1.6 million. Now it was Adam's move, and he sat still with a pair of tens in his hand, believing he had the best hand, putting Alan on two over cards, more than likely an Ace-King or Ace-Queen.

He wasn't Houdini. He drew his assessment from instinct, from years of playing, and from his experience with Alan and the basic math. The chances of Alan having a pocket pair in heads-up poker was less than six percent and a higher pair less than four percent, so his bet illustrated an attempt to trap Adam.

Adam had three choices. It always came down to the same three choices—call, fold, or raise. It made an incredibly complicated game simplistic, with so many variables at play that the infinite possibilities came down to three choices. Adam knew if Alan had Ace-King, he had a thirteen percent advantage. If they were suited, an eight percent advantage. Those odds ran through his mind with quickness and clarity. Dissecting the numbers wasn't even a conscious effort. It was immediate, as ingrained in him as the English language.

The irony was that it took him longer to search for words than numbers. He knew Alan's play. If he raised, Alan would push his chips all in, which was what he wanted. Adam chose a different course of action. He called the $1.6 million, leaving Alan unsure if he was slow playing or bluffing. Either way it didn't give him any information.

The dealer slowly burned a card, then turned three cards over spreading them out, which in Texas hold'em was referred to fondly as "the flop." Ace of hearts, king of diamonds, ten of diamonds—a tremendous flop. The audience looked on. There were so many possibilities.

Adam showed no emotion. He knew if Alan had an ace and a king, his two pair couldn't beat his three tens. "Trips," as they were called, gave him an eighty percent chance of winning.

Alan did what any player would do with two top pair in a heads-up match. He pushed all in, then jumped to his feet taunting, yelling, daring Adam to call.

Alan was talking at Adam, but he wasn't listening. Ignoring his opponent's ridiculous attempts at distraction, he saw only the numbers and the probability. The audience sat in silence, except for Alan's entourage there to support him, who fueled his tirade with applause, feeding the hype. Adam sat motionless, then with a voice loud enough for the dealer and tournament director to hear, he called Alan's bet.

The entire room went quiet with anticipation. Alan was at a loss for words when Adam flipped his cars, showing a pair of tens. He was furious when he realized Adam had three of a kind and his two pairs had less than a twenty percent chance of winning. Alan switched his tactics, breaking the silence, repeating the same phrase over and over, getting his small but loud entourage and supporters to join him in chanting—"Ace, ace,"— attempting to will the ace into existence.

Adam remained in his chair, no expression. The dealer paused, as was the custom to add to the intrigue of televised poker, then slowly burned a card and turned over the ace of diamonds. The fourth card, "the turn," gave Alan a full house—three aces and two kings, otherwise known as aces full of kings.

Alan went berserk as the noise became deafening. His friends screamed along with the shocked reactions of the audience, adding to the unintelligible wall of sound. He went from having a less than twenty percent chance of winning to a ninety-seven percent chance of winning in the flip of a card.

Adam, impervious to the noise and Alan's antics as he took selfies and posted them in real time to his nineteen million followers, waited patiently for the river. Adam knew in that moment, he had "one out," only one card. The last card flipped, "the river," needed to be the last remaining ten—the ten of clubs—and he had a two percent chance, but that wasn't what occupied his mind. He was focused on the fact that he played his hand correctly. Win or lose, the numbers were the only constant equalizer.

While the insanity ensued around him, the dealer milked that last card, and the announcers offered commentary, he switched his thoughts to the similarities between life and poker. The randomness of it, all the variables colliding, creating moments of highs and lows, operating in a controlled set of unchanging rules, eventually coming to an absolute end. Though humans had a role in the choices they made while in the game, they didn't control all the variables and never saw the end until it came.

Everyone had their eyes on the dealer's hands. Alan leaned over the table hands on the rails, while Adam sat in his seat waiting for the final conclusion. The dealer burned the first card, then flipped the last and final card, the two of diamonds, making Alan "The Assassin" Dushku the winner and $987,000 richer.

Alan erupted in a show of bravado, screaming, giving high fives to the gallery, and dragging his entourage into the mix by bringing them down by the table. He had them take pictures while he held a stack of money up to his ear like it was a phone.

Adam rose, acknowledging the congratulatory remarks from those close to the table. Uncomfortable by the scene, he made his way to Alan, interrupted his festivities, congratulated him, and shook his hand.

Alan leaned in and whispered, "Get ready for the same when I see you at the Everest."

Adam ignored the comment, fully aware that in poker the best starting hand didn't always win. He was winning until "the turn," a term that had a dual meaning. In the end, anything could happen regardless of whether a person made the correct choice. No one controlled all the variables.

Adam, accompanied by some tournament officials, made his way to the back office where he verified his banking information. He instructed the back-office personnel that he would like ten thousand in cash and the remainder wired to his bank. Then he walked out to the parking lot, slid behind the wheel of his rented Chevy, and drove the forty-five minutes to Jacksonville International Airport.

He was disappointed that he hadn't won, but it didn't consume him. He was happy with how he played. There was comfort knowing that he hadn't made a mistake. The turn card was unfortunate, but that was poker.

He turned in his rental car, then took the five-minute walk from the rental return across the lanes of people dropping off and picking up friends and family at the main terminal. A smile came to his face when he saw a couple embrace with a kiss—the man wearing Army fatigues, the woman holding the hand of what looked like a three-year-old. Adam could only imagine the sacrifice the couple had endured and assumed there would be more separation in the future.

He was lucky. Only an hour to wait before his flight. The plan was to clear security, find a pub, and grab a bite to eat and a beer while he waited. Fortunately there was a short line. He took his ticket from the pocket of his sweatshirt, then pulled the money clip from the front pocket of his jeans to retrieve his driver's license, and shuffled through four credit cards, a bank card, and a blank business card he kept with him for emergency phone numbers.

No driver's license? He shuffled through a second time. Still no license. Annoyed, he stepped to the side and let people pass him. He tore apart his bag and laptop case looking for his ID. Still no driver's license. He walked back to the waiting area and took a seat in one of the oversized chairs, trying to remember when he had used it last. It had been when he paid for the tournament registration, which was after he had checked into the hotel. Frustrated, he called his contact at the casino and asked if he could check all the usual places for his ID, including the lost and found.

Adam wracked his brain, trying to think of a way to produce identification quickly. He could go online and order another license, but that meant being stuck in Jacksonville for a minimum of two more days, possibly longer. He hated Jacksonville. It was full of the kind of memories he clung to in equal ratio to the ones he tried to forget.

It wasn't long before his phone rang. Jim, his contact from the cardroom, informed him with great remorse that his ID had in fact been located the day before. However, there had been a miscommunication and it was mailed to the address listed on the license.

Adam thanked him and hung up, frustrated with himself for losing his license. He then collected his belongings and headed back to the rental car section, across the traffic lanes he had passed minutes ago. His plan was to rent a large, comfortable SUV for the drive to New Orleans. It was a great excuse for him to enjoy a plate of crawfish etouffee and spend some time with Miss Mabel, Clayton, and Caliste at his home in the Big Easy. He could easily have his ID delivered there, then fly back to Arizona.

The drive would take about seven, maybe eight hours depending on the weather, and he'd made the drive so many times before, it was second nature. This would be a great opportunity to relax, listen to one of his audiobooks, and clear his head before returning home to Lizzy and the kids.

While in line waiting at the rental counter, he texted his assistant, Paul, and had him order a new driver's license and have it expedited to the house in New Orleans.

CHAPTER 2

WAFFLE HOUSE

Adam called Lizzy to explain what happened at the airport. He could hear the irritation in her voice. She was a patient woman, but there had been too many delays over the years. Lizzy had grown numb to the disappointment. This time might have been legit, but the promises and changed plans were far too common. At times she felt like a single parent. Adam's job required heavy traveling, and she was tired of doing it all on her own.

It was always the same argument. He had to make a living to support her and the kids. She always countered with, "I didn't marry you to be alone. We're supposed to be a team, doing life together." Adam apologized as always, promising to ease up on the travel. That was his typical response to end the argument. He would try, but his effort would come in waves, void of consistency. There were times when he was in attendance for every family gathering and the kids' sporting events. Other times he missed them all. What she wanted was to count on him, but too often she settled for what she could get.

Both hung up the phone disappointed, but for entirely different reasons. Their emotions were colliding with the reality of their life. It had become the norm, and neither knew how to change it.

Hunger broke Adam from the randomness of his thoughts. Realizing he was about to be stuck with fast food for the next four hundred miles, he scanned the exit signs for restaurants. Waffle House three miles away. That was a no-brainer. Cheesy eggs, grits, raisin toast, and waffles—the food and nostalgia made it worth stopping.

Adam found a parking space close to the window so he could keep an eye on the rental, then grabbed his laptop, put his coat over the suitcase, and headed for the door. The temperature had to be in the low-seventies, comfortable except for the constant smothering humidity hanging in the air. He then heard yelling behind him. Everything was dark except for the light coming from inside the restaurant, so he moved quickly toward the door. Jacksonville was still the South regardless of the number of Northeasterners who had invaded it for retirement. Guns were plentiful, they didn't suffer fools, and a stray bullet was not on Adam's agenda.

He picked the farthest booth from the door with his back to the wall, as was his custom. He wanted a clear view of the entrance to see people coming and going, no surprises. What was it about not wanting anyone behind him in public spaces? Where did the need come from? Was it innate? Maybe it was fear or the need to observe his surroundings, or maybe he was just weird, but comfort came in the safety he felt knowing no one was behind him.

The belief was that seeing anything unusual coming his way gave him a chance, the ability to plan and react accordingly. He got like this when he was hungry—introspective, consumed with trying to understand the why in everything.

The waitress was nice, taking his order with a smile. Four eggs scrambled with cheese, raisin toast, and a waffle with extra butter.

Adam settled into a warm cup of coffee, reading the latest news on his phone. When the bell rang, announcing a new customer, he looked up. A man just under six foot tall, thin, wearing a baseball cap, jeans, well-worn sneakers, and a flannel shirt walked toward the register. The average-size backpack slung over his shoulder looked to be the only item he was carrying.

He could overhear the man explaining that he had no money, that a stranger had taken the little bit he had and drove away. He just needed to use the restroom, but the hostess kept repeating the policy that it was for paying customers only.

Adam remembered what it was like to be treated less than human, when simple kindness or genuine compassion meant so much. Having no idea who the man was, he interrupted their conversation and asked if the stranger would like to join him for dinner. Then he asked for the bathroom key and got a smile from the relieved teenage cashier.

In a quiet voice, the man thanked Adam and took the key from his outstretched hand. Adam returned to his table, signaling the waitress with a polite tilt of the hand while mouthing, "More coffee."

The waitress came and freshened his coffee, and he explained he would have another guest joining him and they needed a menu. Several minutes later, the man exited the restroom, dropped the key off to the hostess, and started toward the door.

Adam jumped up and approached him. "I thought you were joining me for dinner?"

"I really appreciate you helping me with the restroom," he said. "It was incredibly kind of you, but I don't have money to spend on a meal."

Adam smiled. "No, it's my treat. I'm alone. You would be doing me a favor. I can use the company. I have a long, lonely journey ahead."

The man thanked him and followed him to the table, where a hot cup of coffee and a menu sat waiting for the stranger.

Before sitting down, Adam stuck out his hand. "It's a pleasure to meet you. What's your name?"

"Jacob. Pleased to make your acquaintance. Thanks for what you did back there."

His voice seemed familiar. Had they met before? His face awakened a memory, but it was just out of reach. He couldn't place it.

Jacob gave him a smile that carried effort.

Adam searched for an icebreaker. "Order whatever you'd like. I'm an All-Star-Special kind of guy—a waffle, eggs, toast, grits—but of course there has to be cheese in the eggs."

"Thank you, that sounds good."

Adam observed him, utilizing one of the gifts that had made him so successful at the poker table. Jacob wore clean clothes that were relatively new, his hands were clean and nails clipped, and his teeth were well kept. He certainly hadn't been living on the street. He was clean shaven, and a recent haircut was obvious by the trimmed cut beneath the band of his baseball cap. The backpack he carried could maybe hold two or three sets of clothes and a few personal items. Aside from his skinny appearance, he didn't display the usual characteristics of a street person, at least not one who had lived the life long. Of course, this was all conjecture based on observation, so he needed to ask questions to learn about the man.

"Do you live here in Jacksonville or just passing through?" Jacob asked, pulling him from his thoughts.

"Passing through. I spent the last week here, and honestly I'm looking forward to putting this place in my rearview mirror. How about you? Is Jacksonville your home, or is this a stop along the way to somewhere else?"

Jacob glanced up, making eye contact with Adam for the first time.

Definitely. He'd seen Jacob somewhere before. His eyes were too familiar, and the goose bumps that rose on Adam's arms confirmed his suspicion. The eyes seemingly contained the events of his life—his history that led him to a free meal with a stranger, while carrying everything he owned. If the eyes were the mirrors to the soul, Jacob's eyes had a life written across them that could only be defined as painful.

"No, actually I'm from everywhere and nowhere." After a suppressed laugh—the first sign that the ice was beginning to break—he said just as quietly, "For the past year I've been living in Jacksonville. I was born in Houston but spent most of my childhood bouncing around the world with my father, who was in the oil business. I guess if I called anyplace home, it would be Austin."

Adam sat listening, not sure what to ask next. So many questions came to mind, but he held back, letting Jacob talk. "You've been living in Jacksonville. So are you headed somewhere else?" he asked when Jacob finished.

Jacob set down his coffee, deliberately taking a moment longer than necessary. It seemed he was debating how much he wanted to share with a stranger he'd met less than fifteen minutes earlier. "Austin, or at least I was headed to Austin. Now I'm not sure. I may be staying here in Jacksonville. Circumstances intervened, changing my plans drastically. I'm not sure where I'm going from here, but it'll all work out in the end. God may not always give us the *why*, but he will give us the how, when, where, and who. The *why*... well, that belongs to him."

Adam's stomach dropped, the butterflies falling to his feet. He knew that phrase. Then it all came together at once, the words spilling from his mouth before he could stop. "The Preacher."

A flush tinged Jacob's gaunt cheeks. He looked down at his bag in the same way Adam had seen thousands of poker players debating whether to fold or go all in.

"I'm sorry. I thought I recognized you when you sat down, but I couldn't place you. We met in Covington, Alabama, after you gave the best sermon I ever heard. To this day, no one has even come close. Afterward, you were kind in taking the time to speak with me, shake my hand, and give me encouragement."

As Jacob looked up from his bag, Brenda the waitress's voice broke the moment. "You all look hungry. I got everything here for you." She placed the plates on the table, dropping the extra butter in front of Adam, then excused herself. She returned moments later and smiled as she filled their cups, then told them to just holler if they needed anything else.

imagine. Those we recognize in heaven—the interactions we have with them—will be void of the scar tissue that exists in some of our relationships. The battles within ourselves that consist of fear, pain, anger, resentment, guilt, or shame that we feel and hide in many of our relationships will be washed away. The emotion that occupies our flesh will be gone, replaced with unconditional love—*agape*, a peace that is undefinable by words or human explanation."

Adam took it all in, admiring the brilliance of Jacob's intelligence. Even his eight-year-old son Theo would understand it. He had never thought of it that way, always praying that his cherished relationships would exist in heaven as they did on earth. He'd never considered that those relationships that were broken, or in some cases shattered, either as the result of his choices or failures, would be renewed in love. Often Adam thought of those already in heaven and hoped for an opportunity to apologize for the wrongs he committed. His thoughts concluded with an undeniable truth: they knew forgiveness, having received it from God, and understood the hypocrisy of withholding it from others. The idea of not forgiving would have been washed away with their flesh.

The conversation paused for a bit as they settled into the mile markers passing. The rain turned from an annoying drizzle to a constant downpour that required focused concentration. The sound of the acoustic music continued to play without interruption or static, the gift of satellite radio.

It brought back memories of the last time Adam saw Jacob O'Shea and the trip back from Covington, Alabama. His tape player was broken, and the greatest challenge on his drive home was finding consistent non-staticky radio stations to occupy the time. There were moments when he gave up and sat in silence, pondering sermons The Preacher had delivered, ingraining the biblical knowledge into his memory. It was a time in his life when he was hungry for the things of God.

Now, almost twenty years later, The Preacher sat next to him on a road trip. Adam so badly wanted to ask him what had happened, but he knew that some things you didn't ask. Jacob's last twenty years was his story to tell, in his own way. Only then would it be his pure perception of the experience. If Jacob wanted to explain, he could when and how he chose without the prodding of unsolicited questions.

When Adam looked over, Jacob was asleep. There was a gentle peace in his stillness, and he had the feeling Jacob hadn't found comfort in sleep for a long time. He continued driving, careful to not disturb his passenger. Only 260 miles until they reached New Orleans, a city deep rooted in its complex history and traditions. The Crescent City, the Big Easy, was unlike any other city. Its food, culture, and personality couldn't be duplicated anywhere else in the world. Adam had eaten at restaurants outside Louisiana that attempted to mimic the Cajun flavors. To the untrained palate they were successful, but to anyone who'd ever eaten crawfish etouffee produced in the kitchens of Atchafalaya, it was at best an honorable attempt.

Adam had a long relationship with the city. Like a first love, it had taken him to the heights of joy and depths of despair. The more the miles fell away, the more the memories awoke inside him. Some of the biggest cash games he had ever played took place in the Big Easy—not in the Harrah's that sat on Canal Street or the riverboats that permanently docked along the Mississippi. It was the private games in the mansions of the Garden District, where old money reigned and admittance required an invitation.

The first time Adam was invited to play, he jumped at the opportunity partly out of ambition but mostly out of curiosity. He'd heard whispers about these games in poker rooms from Macau to Las Vegas. It was at his first game that he met the man who would become his mentor, his guide into a world of wealth and access—the kind of lifestyle that films tried to bring to life for their viewers. They succeeded in creating entertainment and envy but never actually achieved the goal of authenticity. Hollywood could duplicate the visual aspects of luxury, but the emotions, style of communication, idiosyncrasies, and unwritten code that couldn't be illustrated in film it had to be taught and lived.

The memories came in waves. The fond memories first, as always. The ones that were held onto after the bad ones were trapped with time, hidden away in the mind's dark vault. He hadn't thought about Jack in a long time. Jack Broussard, the quintessential picture of a Southern aristocrat, his money dating back to the original French colonists. Those French settlers had founded New Orleans in 1718, almost a hundred years before Jefferson made the Louisiana Purchase, paying Napoleon $15 million, a steal at $18 a square mile.

Jack was a chameleon—who he needed to be when it best suited his purposes. Only a handful of people truly knew him and could see that he was not as he intended. Adam was one of those people, really the only one outside his immediate family and a few lifelong friends. Jack made New Orleans come alive for him. It was nearly impossible to visit N'awlins and not feel the magnitude of Jack's presence.

Adam replayed the memory of their first meeting in his mind, as he had many times before. The players were arriving—nine in total, refreshments were given in the salon, and everyone was standing in separate groups waiting for the start.

It felt like high school to Adam, who stood alone by the huge ornate fireplace, sipping a soda water with lime and pretending to admire a grotesquely gaudy clock that sat atop the mantel. He was the new guy, the outsider, the player who they assumed was a "fish"—an inexperienced player. The player they all hoped would leave the game empty-handed and confused, wondering how he lost $500,000.

But Adam would not be the fish. He was the shark, and by the end of the evening the players who had been ignoring him and chatting in their little cliques would wonder how it happened. How did this new kid, through the course of the evening and into the night, separate them from their money so methodically?

He was staring at the clock, lost in his thoughts, when the man standing next to him spoke. He was dressed in a dark-blue suit tailored to his athletic frame, a crisp white dress shirt jumped from the lapels in contrast, and his salt-and-pepper hair was a bit longer than most, his face clean shaven, and his eyes ice blue. He stuck his right hand out to shake, while his left was occupied by what Adam recognized as a strong smoky scotch. His hands were void of any jewelry accept a Paul Newman Daytona Rolex. The classic piece made a statement void of flash, and told anyone who knew what it was that they were dealing with a connoisseur of the finer things.

"Welcome to the party, Mr. Foster. My name is Jack Broussard," he began. "I want to welcome you to my home and thank you for accepting my humble invitation to join us this evening. I apologize for the delay. We will begin momentarily. Just awaiting the arrival of our last guest."

"You have a beautiful home. And please call me Adam. I appreciate the invitation. It's a true honor."

Jack smiled and gave a slightly mischievous laugh. "Call me Jack, but let's wait until the end of the evening to determine whether it was much of an honor. I can assure you, however, it will be entertaining."

Jack's words proved to be true. The night would end with Adam receiving nearly $3 million in winnings wired to his account the following day. Jack walked away with half that amount, not a bad payday for nine hours of work. The game ended at around four a.m., and by the time the car dropped Adam at his hotel, the sun was starting to break the night's grip.

He remembered wondering if he would ever be invited back. They had hoped to hook a fish but wound up catching a shark. Aside from general acknowledgement, no one at the table really spoke to him. Adam spent the evening listening to the banter between players, observing their betting, looking for tells, and winning. The more he thought about it, his intention was never to find friends, it was to make money. He already had friends.

Adam showered, trying to wash away the grimy feeling of a late-nighter before collapsing into bed. His intention was to remain there until it was time to leave for his five p.m. flight, but those plans were interrupted by a knock at the door. Scared one of the players was angry about their losses, Adam stood to the side of the frame leaning over to look through the peephole. He was surprised to find Jack standing at the door dressed in a different suit and shirt, wide awake as though the day was just starting instead of ending.

Adam hardly knew the man, yet he opened the door and watched as Jack walked past him into the room. There was energy in his voice, excitement, as he said, "Listen, kid. There are opportunities in life. Sometimes we seize them, but oftentimes we wave as they pass by. Later we experience the regret of 'could this have been' and 'what if,' wondering if we watched an opportunity slip away."

He turned around and looked directly at Adam. "This is one of those rare times. I'm giving you two simple choices, both of which will have a direct impact on the rest of your life. You can spend the remainder of the day tucked away in your cozy little bed or you can pack your belongings and meet me downstairs in fifteen minutes. I'll wait for you in the lobby. Fifteen minutes, not one minute more. If you're not there, I'll have your answer." Jack then walked past him and out the door, making his refusal to answer any clarifying questions perfectly clear.

Adam wondered what would have happened if he didn't accept Jack's offer—if he locked the bolt on the door and crawled back into bed. Later those events were made much clearer to him, but in the moment, he chose to see where Jack's invitation took him. On that day, Jack took him to a private airport just outside the city where they boarded a jet. It wasn't until they were in the air that Adam asked, "Where we headed?"

Jack sat across from him, sipping on his drink. "Kid, that's easy. Today, Vegas. Where our journey takes us after Vegas, that's a far more interesting question."

Adam could tell Jack was the kind of guy who took joy in being the only one who knew how all the pieces fit together. Later he would realize that what Jack loved most was controlling the experience, seeing surprise and awe in the naïve and innocent. He enjoyed watching as their beliefs were transformed and corrupted.

CHAPTER 4

WELCOME TO THE BIG EASY

Jacob woke up and took a drink from his water bottle. "Sorry I fell asleep on the job. I'm supposed to keep you company. How long until we reach New Orleans?"

"We're about one hundred miles out. I'm glad you got some sleep though. How you feeling?"

Jacob was drinking again. "Good," he said when he finished. "You know I never asked, what were you doing in Jacksonville? You said it wasn't a place you wanted to be. Were you there for work?"

Adam's profession didn't embarrass him, but he often hesitated to discuss it, especially with strangers. It was a unique occupation, and most people had preconceived notions of what it was to be a professional poker player. "I was there for work competing in a poker tournament." He knew a second question would be coming, so he continued, "I've been a professional poker player for almost twenty years."

Jacob put his water back in the cup holder. "Do you enjoy your job? Does it bring you happiness? Obviously it pays you extraordinarily well, but do you love it?"

Adam thought for a moment. That was a question he hadn't asked himself in years. "Poker is what I do for a living. Fortunately it provides financial freedom for my family. It's comfortable for me. I don't know that I love it, but I'm good at it." Hoping to change the subject, he asked, "How about you? Are you still preaching, doing ministry work?"

"No, I haven't spoke from the pulpit in well over ten years. I still do ministry work but not as a pastor. I work mostly with the homeless and in street ministry. My goal is to reach those who have been abandoned by society or lost in the world of prostitution and substance abuse, remind them that God loves them. Sometimes it pays but most of the time it doesn't. It sounds crazy to most people, but God always provides for my needs."

Adam admired his dedication and reliance on God's provision, but at the same time he questioned the narrative. There was more to the story. He had heard the slight emotional inflexion in Jacob's voice when he said the word *pastor*. He wasn't going to push the subject though.

That type of work required a special person. Society ignored the less fortunate, those who lived on the street. They made assumptions hidden behind ridiculous excuses such as they need to get a job, homelessness is a decision, if you're hungry there's places to eat, addiction is the user's fault, and prostitution is a choice. It was easier to ignore the problem and justify lack of action by blaming the victims for their circumstances. The irony was that the Christians who made those comments were ignoring one of the fundamental principles of being a follower of Christ. Jesus said, "Love your neighbor as yourself." That's what Jacob was doing.

Adam thought of the hypocrisy that often dominates our world. He did not judge those less fortunate, but his silence on the subject and failure to act was participation by omission. "Is there a job for you in Austin continuing your street ministry?" he asked. "That city is expanding quickly and housing prices are skyrocketing, so I assume the homeless population is as well."

"Actually, I'm headed to Austin to say goodbye to an old friend," Jacob said. "I haven't seen him in a long time. I want to capture some memories before he's gone."

Adam could relate. "I missed saying goodbye to a few of the family members I loved the most. Now I live with the pain, anger, and, in my case, shame for allowing it to happen."

Jacob glanced at him. "The pain and anger are understandable, but shame? Where's that come from?"

Adam had never been one to share his innermost thoughts and feelings, especially when the topic was so sensitive. His first reaction was to ignore the question, but this was Jacob O'Shea. Even though he didn't consider himself a pastor anymore, he was still The Preacher. And Lizzy was always complaining that Adam internalized too much and never shared his true thoughts and feelings. Maybe he needed to work on that. "When I started doing well, making real money, I included some of my family in the financial wave and money changed hands. I enjoyed their newfound interest in me, and I was achieving what I thought was success, the kind of success they understood. At the time, I defined success as money, jewelry, cars, houses, travel, access, and opportunity. The more the better until the perfect storm came, washing it all away, leaving me financially and emotionally shattered."

He drew a breath and shook his head. "I didn't know how to tell them it was all gone, that I made some poor decisions. That there were some events completely outside of my control. Ultimately, I was a coward and didn't want to deal with the fallout. I said nothing and allowed them to believe whatever narrative they chose. The reality is that in the absence of truth people will make up their own, especially if there are people around them driven by drama, that pour fuel on the fire. There is much more to the story—a complicated history, as there often is with these things. We haven't spoken in over fifteen years. I love them and miss them, but I'm a completely different person now. They wouldn't recognize me. They wouldn't believe who I am now is real, and they definitely wouldn't understand."

Jacob sat in silence for a few moments. "I'm guessing they live in Jacksonville?"

Adam took his eyes off the road for a second. "Close. Farther down the coast in St. Augustine. I grew up in South Jersey, just across the bridge from Philly. My family moved after I left home. My two brothers, Mom, Dad, and later my grandfather went to Florida."

"Have you tried to reconnect? Reached out to them with an apology?"

This wasn't a conversation Adam wanted to have with anyone. He shifted in his seat. "In the words of Shakespeare, 'what's done cannot be undone.' So much has happened since then."

"I'm sorry. I didn't mean to be nosey."

"No, it's all good. Just a topic better left to the passing of time."

When they reached New Orleans, Adam pulled off I-10 onto I-90, then took it a short distance to St. Charles Avenue and the Garden District. He turned into the well-known driveway that passed to the left of the old Victorian mansion, finally parking in front of the two-car garage with an apartment above it. Beyond the garage, the lawn looked the same—riddled with flower beds and bird baths.

It was now just past seven a.m., and although Jacob had gotten some much-needed sleep, Adam had driven through the night. Sleep was his number one priority.

When Adam got out of the car, Caliste was already standing there waiting for him. He looked the same as ever—light skin, average height, and thin, with dark-green eyes and a natural wave to his hair. "You've got to be exhausted. Come on in the house. Leave your bags. I'll have Clayton take them up to your rooms." He offered his hand to Jacob. "I'm Caliste. You must be Jacob. It's good to meet you. I've heard a lot about you."

Jacob shook his hand. "All good things, I hope."

"Of course."

Adam and Jacob followed him up the walkway and onto the back porch. In the kitchen, fresh beignets from Café Du Monde, the world-renowned French market, sat on the counter.

"I know you're exhausted, but help yourself to a couple before you sleep. Miss Mabel picked these up special for you this morning."

Adam thanked him with a thumbs up since a beignet was already in his mouth. They took seats at the table in the kitchen, and Caliste poured a steaming chicory coffee blend into their cups.

"Where's Miss Mabel?" Adam asked. Caliste's grandmother was considered one of the best cooks in all the parishes. No one knew her age or dared to ask, but Adam figured she had to be in her nineties. A true creole woman, she still had the beauty of her youth in her emerald-green eyes and was as tough as a coffin nail with a heart of gold.

Caliste poured more coffee in his cup. "Out picking up all your favorites, and probably has half the city traffic slowed to a crawl. She refuses to go the speed limit. If she's doing ten under, it's a miracle. I tried to get her to pick one store close by, but that was a mistake. The back of my head still hurts from where she hit it with the cooking spoon."

All three men were laughing when Clayton came into the kitchen. He introduced himself to Jacob, then gave Adam a bear hug. At about six foot four and more than three hundred pounds, Caliste's right-hand man was an imposing presence but a gentle giant.

Caliste poured him a cup, and Clayton sat down with them. "How was your trip? The weather looked pretty rough on the news last night."

Adam shrugged. "There were a few moments I considered pulling off the road for a break, but most of the way it was just steady rain."

When they finished their coffee, Clayton put his cup in the sink and headed outside.

Caliste stood up as well. "Gentleman, I'll be in the front study if you need me for anything."

"If I'm not up by two, please come knock on my door," Adam said.

He stopped at the doorway and grinned. "Sure. But I'm thinking the smell of Miss Mabel's redfish courtbouillon and gumbo will be your alarm clock."

Once the two were gone, Jacob looked at Adam. "I can't thank you enough. You've been a blessing. I don't want to overstay my welcome, so I should probably be on my way to Austin."

"Why don't you stick around, join me, be my guest?" Adam said. "Relax and have some of the best cooking you'll ever have in your life. This evening I'm going to enjoy the city before I leave for home tomorrow. I can have Caliste get you on a flight to Austin tomorrow afternoon."

Adam took the $10,000 in cash from his laptop bag, then placed it on the table between them. "This is a gift to help you get started. It's a blessing, so please don't try to argue with me. I don't want you to feel pressured to stay, but if you want to, your room is up the stairs, third door on the right. If not, I completely understand. Either way the money is yours." He got up. "Take your time. Enjoy the coffee and beignets. If you decide to leave, just let Caliste know. He'll make the arrangements and Clayton will give you a lift to the airport."

Jacob's smile was genuine. "Thank you. You've done so much already. I don't know what else to say."

Adam grinned and headed for the door. "Say you'll stay."

He walked through the formal dining room into the large salon, then turned down a hallway past the stairs, a powder room, and the downstairs bedroom before sliding apart the two large doors that opened to the front study.

Caliste sat in one of the two oversized leather chairs that faced each other with a dark cherry table between them. Across the room was a massive desk, and behind it a large window that gave a full view of the front yard. Amid the walls decorated with built in bookshelves that left enough room between them for antique framed maps, photographs, and old paintings of the cityscapes, Caliste looked up from his cellphone and placed it on the table.

Adam took the seat across from him. "Listen, my friend. I need you to find out everything you can about Jacob. I'd like to know where he's been for the past fifteen plus years. I'm pretty sure he's sick. Cancer, I think, going by his symptoms. Reach out to Liam for the background check. Also, if you find out he's sick, have Liam get an appointment with the best oncologist on the West Coast. If he asks for when, tell him the day after tomorrow would be ideal. Ask him to get all his medical records and to make sure the doctor has them in time for the appointment." Liam and Adam weren't blood, but they were family, their friendship having been forged in a tragedy that occurred in the very room where they sat.

Caliste nodded. "You know I saw The Preacher at Pastor Givens' church with Miss Mabel years ago, one of the most powerful sermons I've ever heard. She still believes he's the greatest preacher she's ever heard. Where did you find him?"

"A Waffle House in Jacksonville. He was in a bad way, so I offered him a meal. I didn't realize who he was until later."

"Are you sure you want to know where he's been?" Caliste eyed him. "Look, it's none of my business, but if you're trying to build a friendship, doing a background check on him is a tremendous violation of his privacy. Maybe you should just ask him? You know I'll do whatever you ask, but you made me swear a long time ago to ask the hard questions."

Caliste was right about the invasion of privacy, but Jacob's health was failing, Adam could feel it. The other stuff—where he'd been all this time, what he'd been doing—wasn't his primary concern. "I'm not here to judge him," Adam said. "Lord knows, and you know, I'm the last person who should judge anyone. I need to help him. I know he's in pain. I can't explain how, but I know it in my core."

Caliste nodded. Not that he had another choice. Adam was not only his friend but also his boss and the owner of the house.

"Also, let's make sure he has some suitable clothing and a suit for the evening. Any suggestions on entertainment for tonight? I would really like to decompress before heading home. Which reminds me, can you also pick up a Bvlgari bracelet for Lizzy, something with diamonds?"

Caliste laughed. "What did you do to piss her off this time?"

Adam didn't reply.

"It's Fat Tuesday. There's a whole lot to do, and tonight's going to bring out all kinds of crazy in the quarter."

How had he forgotten? "I didn't even realize it was Mardi Gras. I might have kept driving all the way to San Antonio. Okay. Well, if we're going to have to deal with that insanity, we might as well have a front-row seat. Line up something tonight that includes balconies on Bourbon Street. Invite the right people so no one's offended. If I'm stuck doing this, let's get some benefit out of it. Reward those who have been a resource, and invite anyone we anticipate being of benefit in the future. Make sure to invite Ramos Copperwood. I know he's out of town, but make the gesture. It's not a good idea to offend your all-star attorney, even if he is a friend."

"I'll take care of it. Get some rest."

Adam lifted himself from the chair like a man twice his age, using the arm rests for leverage. At the door, he turned around. "Tell Liam I would have called but I'm exhausted. Let him know this is important to me. The sooner he knows something, the better."

———

Caliste sat in the study organizing his priorities. He needed to call Liam, pick up the bracelet, and get some clothes for Jacob. Also, finding a venue on such short notice, even with his connections, would be no easy task. He and Clayton would make the rounds as soon as he finished the call with Liam.

Caliste had seen a vulnerability in Adam that he hadn't seen in years. He was letting someone in, taking a chance, which was out of character. Adam hadn't let anyone into his inner circle for as long as Caliste had known him.

He knew he was procrastinating. Dealing with Liam Callahan always made him uncomfortable. Liam was a fixer, employing whatever means necessary to accomplish the goal. The moral compass needle swung in circles when he was involved, making Caliste nervous every time they crossed paths. He had witnessed the man's work firsthand, and his skills were undeniable. Liam could not only see all the angles in any given scenario, he could quantify all the outcomes in his head simultaneously. The man was terrifyingly gifted, brilliant really, but he lacked empathy.

Finally, Caliste picked up his phone and dialed Liam's number.

After a few rings, Liam answered. "Well, hello, *cher*. It's been a while. How are things in the Big Easy?"

Knowing he called him *cher*—the Cajun term for *dear*—to get a reaction, Caliste refused to acknowledge it. "Our friend is in town, and he needs your help with a few things."

Liam got serious. "Give me the details."

He filled him in on Adam's request, then finished, "Look, I saw this guy preach. It was mind blowing—he has a gift—but obviously things have changed since then. I don't want to see Adam get hurt. We don't know this guy or the extent of his baggage."

He grunted. "I'll make sure no stone is left unturned. Let me deconstruct his past fifteen years. Let's be diligent in the meantime. Make sure Clayton is around in case things go sideways. If anything strange happens, call me—day or night."

Caliste laughed. "You mean like Adam picking up a stranger at Waffle House, driving him nearly five hundred miles to his home, and giving him a place to stay? Yeah, if anything strange happens, I'll let you know."

CHAPTER 5

MISS MABEL

Jacob opened his eyes. His sleep had been so deep that it seemed like a day had passed. It wasn't a dream. He was waking up in the guest room of a professional poker player's New Orleans mansion. Scanning the room, trying to break the grip of sleep, he found a pile of folded clothes on top of the dresser.

He climbed out of bed, fighting the weakness in his body, then paused a moment and took his time standing. That's when the delicious scent came to him. His sense of smell was nearly gone, so it was a pleasant surprise. It also triggered his appetite, reminding his stomach that it hadn't had a meal since Waffle House.

Next to the clothing was a note:

> *Additional clothes are hanging in the closet.*
> *They're yours. Hope we got the sizes right.*
> *Adam, Caliste, and Clayton*

In the closet Jacob found a gray suit, tie, and dress shirt hanging up. They were his exact size. Even the monk-strap dress shoes on the shelf, size eleven, were perfect. He took a pair of jeans, underwear, a T-shirt, and a pullover from the pile. He let the shower water run hot and shut the bathroom door to capture the steam. Wiping it from the mirror with a towel, he stared at his reflection. His body was a skeleton of its former self, but he thanked God that his mind and faith remained whole.

Jacob stood steadfast in his faith. After his life being splintered into a million pieces, being scared and bankrupt, he never lost his trust in God. The pain of betrayal came from those he believed to be his friends—pastors, men of God who refused to help him without receiving something in return. A few had helped him survive a week or two, but many listened to his dire straits, then simply offered prayers or an invitation to come and preach. He couldn't even get out of bed, let alone travel or deliver a sermon. Even now the forgiveness he forced toward those who abandoned him began to creep back into his conscience. He quickly focused on the present and all the gifts God had supplied. A warm, comfortable bed, a shower, clothes, transportation, money, and the smell of a homecooked meal drew him out of self-pity.

By the time he finished showering and getting dressed, the antique clock on the wall said it was half past noon. Jacob followed the aroma down to the kitchen.

Sitting at the kitchen table, an older woman—skinny, her deep-green eyes focused on him—smiled. The intensity of her gaze was so unnerving that he wanted to look away, but he couldn't. Her stillness was mesmerizing.

"Child, I have been waiting for you," she said. "Come on and sit down." She pointed at the seat next to her.

Although still unnerved, he sat down and folded his hands on the table. He could still feel her stare and tried not to make eye contact, but he couldn't help it.

"Everybody calls me Miss Mabel. Pleased to meet you." Without waiting for his response, she continued, "I took Caliste to see you preach at Pastor Givens' church in LaPlace. He wasn't happy 'bout it, put on such a holla, but once he heard your message, he thanked me on the drive back home. Now God has you sitting in my kitchen. Even at my age, he still surprising me."

She placed one of her weathered hands over his folded ones. "I was raised by my grandparents not but ten miles from this house we sitting in now. They was good solid hardworking folk. The only time they stopped was to eat or sleep. I watched them build something out of nothing. It wasn't much, just a small restaurant, but people came from all around these parts. We lived in a small one-room shack bout twenty-five paces from the back of the restaurant. They was my mama's parents. She died in childbirth bringing me into this world. My father said he wasn't raising a little girl in them days, so he left. I never saw or heard from him again. Years later I got a telegram from his sister telling me he died, caught up on the wrong side of the law."

Miss Mabel stood up. Jacob had no idea where she was going or why she was telling him about her childhood. He watched her pour a huge glass of water, then fill a cup with coffee. Before he had a chance to get his own, she slid the large glass of water in front of him.

He took a long drink, and when he was finished, she continued her story as if she never stopped. "Child, my grandparents, they was good God-fearing, church-going people, raised me up the same. They used what little they had with wisdom, gave whatever they could spare to those that had nothing. One day we was out back the restaurant cooking, getting ready to open for the evening, when a big fancy car pulled up. This huge fat man all dressed in a suit that was so tight it spilled out everywhere, gets out the car. He starts talking to my grandpa, doesn't shake his hand or nothing. He says, 'Listen here, boy. I'm going to need you to clear outta here, take your business somewhere else. I'm fittin' to build on this here land a proper bar with good solid eats, which means you're going to be leaving. I'm going to do you a favor. The law says I got to give you this here hundred-dollar bill for your trouble. I figure it's the Christian thing to do, at least that's what's helping me get through this nonsense.' He stuck the hundred-dollar bill out, and when my grandpa walked toward him, the fat man smiled. I ain't never forgotten that smile. It's been stuck in my mind all these years later. I saw the evil, child. You could see the devil in him."

She stopped for a moment and sighed. "When my grandpa got close, the fat man said, 'Get on your knees, boy, and thank me. You're lucky I didn't just burn this dump down with you and your women in it.' My grandpa was up in years, but he was still a strong powerful man beaten and aged with iron. He walked up close to the man and looked him straight in his eyes, which was not something you did in them days. Grandpa didn't turn his eyes away and said, 'Thank you, sir, for wanting to buy my place, but I'm not for sale. This here is my home. I welcome you to some free eats tonight when we open. Now, I ask you to be on your way so I can finish up my cooking. People be coming soon.'

"The fat man's face became the color of hell fire, his eyes bulged from the rage, and you could see the hatred building inside him. He spit in my grandpa's face. My grandpa used the sleeve of his shirt to wipe it away. When he was finished, the man backhanded him, causing blood to stream from his nose. My grandpa said nothing, did nothing but just kept staring into the fat man's eyes as the blood dripped down his chin. The fat man walked backward to his car, not taking his eyes off my grandpa. 'Boy, you going to get a lesson to help you remember your place,' he said. 'If you're not gone when I get back, not even Jesus will be able to save you.'"

She shook her head. "I remember looking up at my grandma when the fat man spun his tires, screeching out onto the road. She was scared to death. I ain't never seen her so filled with fear. She just stood staring at where the argument between the fat man and my grandpa happened, until she felt my arms hugging her waist. She looked down at me and tried to smile as tears rolled down her face." Miss Mabel was reliving the moment, there watching it happen.

Jacob rose, took some tissues from a box on the counter, and handed them to her as he sat back down.

She dabbed the corners of her eyes, then took a deep breath. "You see, my grandma spoke under her breath, 'He done woke the devil now, and he be coming for us.' To this day, child, I don't think she even knew she said the words, but her tongue betrayed her thoughts. I ain't know what that meant. I was only nine years old at the time." A tight smile crossed her thin face. "I can tell you it stayed with me, burned in my memories. Wasn't the words, it was the fear. It was so real, it hung in the air and you could almost see it. She tried talking to grandpa, but he wouldn't hear it. He told her he was tired, they built this outta nothing, the white man took his freedom before, and he ain't never gettin' the chance again. That night they came for us, didn't bother with the hoods."

Miss Mabel dabbed her eyes again. "I woke up from my sleep to the sound of cars pulling into the rocks, headlights coming through my window. The lights in pieces moving from one side of my wall to the other, then gone. Grandma had sent me to bed while they finished cleaning up for the night. I peeked through the window when the lights stopped. The fat man was back, with twenty or twenty-five men standing in the yard between the restaurant and our shack. There was just enough light coming from the small spotlight that hung over the rear door to see."

She stopped to take a sip from her cup and gather her composure. "My grandpa was standing in front of my grandma, his arm out to one side like someone protecting a child or holding back a fighter. The fat man was yelling. This time it was my grandma hollering back at them. I ain't never seen her lose control, she was hollerin' so loud I could hear her through the wall. My grandpa was doing all he could to hold her back. It wasn't long before the men had them both on the ground, kicking, punching, and beating them with bats. I watched them drag my grandpa into the restaurant, and a few minutes later the fat man walked out the door lighting a bottle. He tossed it back inside, and the cowards held my grandma's face up so she could see the place burn with him inside. I watched the fires light cast shadows across Grandma's bloodied face."

Miss Mabel wiped her eyes again, and Jacob did the same with the sleeve of his pullover. He still didn't know why she was telling him the story, but it somehow seemed necessary.

Miss Mabel squeezed his hand. "When they was gone, I ran out to my grandma, fell to the ground, and crawled up beside her. I got as close as I could. She said, 'Baby girl, I'm dying. Ain't no saving me. I knew when that fat devil came, this was my last day on earth. I'm going home, baby, going to be with Jesus. Don't suffer no tears for me. I forgive them for what they do, and you promise me you will too. You promise me, baby, you promise me, you hear, don't let them put no hatred in your heart. Their sin ain't worth it. You pray for them, baby girl.' That's the last thing Grandma said to me before she went on to glory."

She looked him in the eyes. "In my life I have questioned her words, tried to ignore them, ran from them, sometimes out of anger, other times shame. In the end she been right every time, her words are God's promise to us." Her gaze dropped to their entwined hands. "Child, are you running toward something or from something?"

He emptied his glass of water. "Miss Mabel, I'm not running. I'm dying."

She nodded once. "Child, I know your dying, but until you're back behind the pulpit sharing the gift that God gave you, are you running? Everybody's time fittin' to come. We're all dying from the day he breathes life into us. The clock is ticking on all of us. You just know yours will be stopping sooner than later. Your love for the Word hasn't changed. I can feel God's hand on you. Only thing changed is knowing your time is short."

Jacob wished it was that easy, but his time had passed. He no longer possessed the strength. He got up and refilled his water at the

"I know, but what are you waiting on? I see you. I been watching you for eighteen years. I remember the first morning you sat at that table, trying to figure out what's what, like a baby bird whose mama's bringing it food for the first time. Your eyes big as sugar cookies listening to Jack telling you 'bout the world." She nodded once. "I'm looking at you now trying to find your way out the guilt. I done told you, it wasn't your fault. I was there same as you. The past ain't going to change, but your future—what you're doing now, the choices you make now—the past ain't got no claim on."

She held his gaze. "Child, sometimes when we refuse to hear God calling or only listen when it's easy, he puts us at a crossroads. You at a crossroads right now. Jacob's not in this house by chance. Make sure you ain't trying to control the story. You got to let God guide you down his path, the right path. That means you going to have to talk to him. That's what he wants, don't matter what you want. You going to bend to God now or later, but you're fittin' to bend to his purpose in the end."

Adam opened his mouth, but Miss Mabel cut him off. "No, child, ain't nothing else to say. What needs to be said been said. Now help me out this chair. I got tending to do in the kitchen."

As he helped her up, she watched him with the face of a concerned mother unsure of the road her son would take but knowing it was his journey to make. Then she headed for the kitchen.

A few minutes later, Caliste came down the stairs.

"Everything good for tonight?" Adam asked.

Caliste continued tinkering with his pocket square. "Yeah. As soon as they get back, we can go. Everything's ready. It's been a while since you been to The Blue Note. Miles is running things now his dad's semi-retired. Miles said old Lloyd is hanging around just enough to dance on his last nerve."

They both laughed. The Blue Note had been a cornerstone of the jazz scene in New Orleans for the better part of fifty years. Lloyd lived, breathed, and bled jazz, and he'd passed on the love to his son Miles, who became a pretty successful musician in his own right.

"So are you planning to take Jacob home with you? What's the deal with this guy?" Caliste was an employee, but he knew Adam considered him family, so he could ask the tough questions when he needed to.

"There's no agenda. I still believe in God even if I don't go to church. Jacob needed help and it was the right thing to do." He shrugged. "I'm supposed to help Jacob, that I know. These events are too random for chance. In my youth, he helped me find comfort in understanding God's Word, so whatever he needs or wants, if it's possible, I'll make it happen. Who knows. Maybe this will wash away some of my past sins."

Going by Caliste's expression, Adam's explanation couldn't have been a more confused, polluted, inaccurate version of how God works. But he didn't say that. "Whatever you need, I'm in. I always got your back. I haven't heard back from Liam, but we should hear from him in the next few hours. Are you sure you don't want to just ask Jacob if he's sick, what happened to him, where he's been the past twenty years? Liam will get all the facts, there's no question about that, but we have no context. The context is just as important, and Jacob is the only one who can truly supply that."

Adam took another sip of his drink, then stared into the glass. "People lie. They tell you what you want to hear, leaving out important pieces, both good and bad. I don't want a presentation, I want to know the truth. Facts, not some twisted, watered-down version of the events. I'll ask him, but after I know all the answers."

Caliste eyed him. Adam was so busy trying to control everything, he was forgetting to be human. He played life like chess, trying to control every piece with calculated precision, wanting to know how every possible move impacted the game. But life wasn't a game. Adam had become so wrapped up in answering to only himself, that he refused to be questioned. Caliste didn't care, and called out Adam, knowing it wouldn't end well. "What's this about, you or Jacob? Because if it's about Jacob, you would ask him what he needs, how you could help.

He would probably tell you what happened in his own time, not yours. This isn't a game. It's a man's life. If you're going to put yourself in it, you should probably ask if you're invited. I know you want to help and that's commendable—it's one of the things I admire most about you—but you're going about it the wrong way. You're starting this friendship off by betraying him. Is that the foundation you want to build on?"

Adam shook his head, annoyed. "Obviously this is something God wants me to do. Why me, I don't know. I found him broke at a Waffle House. Now he has food, clothes, shelter, and money, so I'm guessing he's better off after meeting me. That would make this about him. Besides, I'm not sure what I'm getting out of the deal other than the bill, and maybe if I'm lucky, some of God's favor for listening?"

"That's the problem," Caliste said. "You're not sure what you're getting. You may get nothing more than the feeling that comes from helping others. God doesn't work like a spreadsheet. You aren't going to wash away some columns by performing a good deed. He isn't obligated to give you anything. Everything you have comes from him. He allowed you to have it, entrusted you with it. This has to be about Jacob. It can't be about gaining something for yourself or receiving redemption for your past."

"I get that, but—"

"If that's your goal, do the man a favor and put him on a plane to wherever he wants to go. This can't be about you. You're so busy running from God's purpose for your life that you're ignoring what you already know. God doesn't give you a checklist. You don't get to pick and choose what part of his Word you want to obey or follow. You of all people know what it means to be all in. If this man has been through all that we think he has, then you better be in this with a heart of faith, not money or a sense of entitlement."

Adam grit his teeth. "Who do you think your talking to? I didn't ask for your counsel or opinion on my relationship with God. If I want your view, I'll ask for it. Otherwise, keep your mouth shut and do what your told."

"Well." Miss Mabel's voice turned them both toward the doorway. She took a step into the room, staring at Adam. "I know you angry, fittin' to believe what you want, but did Caliste say anything wasn't true? He just looking out for you, child, wants what's best for you. We all do." She turned her attention to Caliste. "You could have gone about that better, instead of hitting him upside his head. We aren't *like* family, we *are* family. You was taught better. You going to say something, you say it with love."

Chastised, Caliste stuck out his hand. "My bad. That's on me. I just wanted to make sure you stepped into this with your eyes wide open."

Adam shook his hand and went to the wet bar to pour another drink. He then carried his drink to the front study, leaving the two standing in the salon.

———

As soon as the doors closed down the hall, Miss Mabel grabbed her grandson's hand. "Just leave him be. Looks like he done started on that Irish whiskey. He won't hear anything we got to say. He going to that quiet place in his head, trying to kill his memories with that Irish fire, least for the night."

Caliste nodded. "He doesn't touch a drop when he's playing, but it looks like he's already deep in the bottle. Something's eating at him."

Miss Mabel frowned. "Well, make sure you keep an eye on him tonight. That Irish fire takes him places he don't want to go."

He scowled. "Now that I think about it, he hasn't been here when he wasn't playing since the weekend of Jack's funeral. Maybe that's the problem. His mind's stuck on the past. When his mind's idle, it's too much for him."

She pulled Caliste's face down and kissed him on the cheek. "Baby boy, there's a lot going on that ain't for us to know right now. But I know this, the devil's on Adam's heels. God's been waiting on Adam to open that door so he can get saved."

As Miss Mabel headed back to the kitchen, Caliste took a seat by the fireplace. He would grab as much silence as he could before the night stole it away.

———

In the study, Adam stretched out using the table as a footrest. Still angry, he sipped at his whiskey, allowing it to rest in his mouth. It numbed his tongue, and he swirled it around trapping it with his teeth before swallowing it. He admired the maps that covered the walls, waiting for the drink to numb his brain.

When he was at the poker table, his mind was at rest. He was calculating odds, observing behavior, blocking out external thoughts. Away from the table, the memories flooded his thoughts and the past haunted him with regret.

He sighed, then took another sip and dialed Lizzy's number.

"Hi, Dad!" Theo exclaimed.

Hearing his son's voice made him smile. "Hey, little buddy. Where's Mom?"

"She's having a grown-up talk with Lilly upstairs," he replied, a slight whistle in his voice from the tooth he lost. "I'm supposed to stay down here and wait for them to finish, then we can go to soccer practice."

Grown-up talk. That was what Theo called it whenever he was left out of a conversation or asked to leave the room.

"Where are you, Dad? When're you coming home?"

"In New Orleans. I'll be home tomorrow night, buddy, probably in time for dinner. I miss you. Will you tell Mommy and Lilly I miss them too?"

"Okay, Daddy. Are you with Miss Mabel? She makes the best chocolate milk."

Adam chuckled. If only his life could be so simple. "Yes, I'm with her and Caliste and Clayton. Have a good practice, little buddy. I'll see you tomorrow." He hung up, again realizing how fortunate he was to have two incredible kids and Lizzy, even if Lizzy did get tired of him being gone so much.

His mind back in New Orleans, he couldn't stop focusing on the past, dissecting his choices. Jack could have just as easily been sitting across from him. His presence was there in his memories, his teachings, and the lessons running through Adam's mind. The twisted code of ethics—although situational ethics would be a better term to describe his education. Jack was now gone almost fifteen years, but Adam couldn't forget what he'd learned. He tried, but when he hoped for the best while seeing the worst in situations, what he thought would happen almost always did.

Caliste was right. Adam was holding back, unwilling to give it all to God. The idea of relinquishing control, going "all in" as his Christian friends would say, seemed impossible in his world. How could he play by the rules when no one else did? That would set him up for failure. His mind was running again, and he so badly wanted it to stop.

Glancing down at the empty glass, he headed for the wet bar, hoping more whiskey would wash away the memories.

Chapter 7

Mardi Gras

The Mercedes van made its way through the smothering crowd of debauchery that engulfed the streets. As it crawled through the crowd, people in all stages of dress surrounded it, some intoxicated, some vomiting where they stood. One woman threw up on herself and her drink, the green grenade falling from her grip as she tried to stop the vomit with her hands. The music combined with incoherent voices created a giant wall of sound, the volume so loud that it penetrated the insulated van, saturating the air.

Caliste and Jacob sat facing Clayton and Adam with a small table separating them. They watched through the tinted windows, unable to turn away from the insanity unfolding before their eyes. Mitchell, an Army Ranger turned protection agency owner, drove, stopping often as people made room in the street for the van. He was a friend of Clayton and Caliste dating back to elementary school. He was not a large man—maybe five foot seven and one hundred forty-five pounds. His red hair stood out more than he did in a crowd, but he wasn't to be underestimated. His father was a Navy man, stationed in

New Orleans at the end of his career. Mitchell took a different path, joining the Army straight out of high school, ultimately becoming a Ranger. After serving three tours in Afghanistan, he finished up his service as an instructor, then returned to the Big Easy, the only place he called home. Now he ran his own protection agency for visiting dignitaries and high-profile clients, and was the group's added security for the evening. Caliste wanted to leave nothing to chance, and Mitchell was the best and one of the few people he trusted.

The van pulled into an alley, then stopped directly in front of the rear entrance. Miles stood waiting at the club's back door, and he ushered them inside and through the small kitchen to the elevated VIP section. About five feet higher than the floor, it looked out over the main dance floor that led to the stage. Small tables in different configurations surrounded the dance floor, each positioned to give customers the best possible view of the stage.

The VIP room had a Roaring 1920s feel, with a classic look reminiscent of the clubs popularized during that era. Four large leather chairs sat in a horseshoe shape, each separated by a small table with a lamp providing dim light, and a larger table sitting at the center. Two additional areas with the same configuration extended down the wall, ending at the door to Miles' office. Jacob and Adam sat facing the stage, while Clayton and Caliste faced each other but only had to turn slightly to see the stage. Mitchell stood five feet from them, leaning against the wall near the staircase. His focus was away from them, monitoring the entrances, watching people, and looking for anything that could be a potential threat.

The smooth music created a calming, mellow vibe. Two servers soon appeared and took everyone's order. The Blue Note was known for their minimalistic menu of five Cajun appetizers, plus drinks. They chatted among themselves, but mostly listened to the music.

Miles walked to the stage carrying his trumpet and joined the house band for a few songs, but it was no typical band. He hand-picked the best. There was a reason he had toured with some of the greatest musicians over the past twenty years. Miles had a gift—many would say a talent—but his ability clearly came from God.

———————

Jacob never turned his eyes from the stage, not wanting to miss anything as the music washed over him. It sounded so pure, innocent, and incorruptible that for a moment he wished he was the music. Music existed for a moment in time, a product of its circumstances, delivering an interpretative message before disappearing into the memory of the listener.

Jacob's trance was broken when Miles thanked the audience and then left the stage to a standing ovation. Jacob lifted his glass of water and let it slowly trickle down his throat. The cancer left his throat permanently dry, so he constantly craved fluids. Jacob avoided alcohol—not only did it wear down his already fragile immune system but it also caused dehydration—but Adam obviously didn't. He'd been drinking at the house, and now he had the drinks coming one after the other. The server never left his glass dry.

Adam was obviously intent on drinking as much as possible, and Jacob made a mental note to be careful in conversation. Too many times he'd experienced how even limited quantities of alcohol changed a person's behavior and caused unnecessary confrontation.

Miles made his way through the tables, stopping at each one, shaking hands, and thanking the customers for coming out. It took him a while to get across the room to the VIP section, but once there he gave Mitchell a man hug first, then Caliste, Adam, and Clayton. He stopped at Jacob, and Adam made a formal introduction. Miles stuck his hand out, but Jacob gave him a man hug instead.

Miles laughed off the moment of surprise. "Anyone that is a friend of these brothers is a friend of mine." Miles was tall on the stage, but now standing next to him, Jacob realized he was nearly seven feet tall. He was a skinny man with huge hands and a dark complexion, and he was starting to bald but his height disguised it. Wearing an all-black suit with a slight shine, a black dress shirt with a white collar and white cuffs, and black gators, he was dressed in pure style.

"That performance was amazing," Jacob said. "It's been a long time since I heard proper jazz. It reminded me of the first time I heard Coltrane, the simplistic power of each note, woven into a masterpiece."

"Yeah, there's some definite elements of Coltrane in my sound. He made a tremendous impact on me when I was a kid. I wore those records out, playing them over and over trying to duplicate not just the sound but the feel." Miles was interrupted by one of the servers, and he excused himself to follow the server back through the crowd to the kitchen.

A new act took the stage, a unique combination of blues, jazz, and funk called Grand Fusion. Their music drove couples out of their seats and onto the dance floor. Guests started arriving in the VIP section, and after being cleared by Mitchell they were greeted by Adam and Caliste.

Jacob leaned toward Caliste while Adam talked to one of them. "Who are all these people?"

Caliste jutted his chin at the well-dressed, short, heavy-set bald man speaking to Adam. "That's Walter Hawthorn. His family's been the leading liquor distributor in most of Louisiana since the 1930s. Huey Long, 'The Kingfish' himself, got that deal done. His family has maintained the distribution rights ever since. They have so much political pull, even in the days of Carlos Marcello, his family was left alone. His political connections are steel. No one knows the extent of the family's true wealth."

Jacob laughed. "Okay, but that didn't answer my question. Why is he here? Was he invited?"

"There are nine people who play in the big game every quarter here in N'awlins. Walter is one of them. He's been playing since it started forty years ago. Adam took Jack's permanent place about fifteen years ago. Honestly, he probably has the lowest net worth of all of them, although since the first day he played as a guest, he has won the most money by far with a few noteworthy losses along the way."

Caliste glanced at the man again, then looked back to Jacob. "Adam invited all nine of them as a sign of respect. Just in case he might ever need a favor. If he did, these guys have the power to make almost anything happen in the state of Louisiana. There's rich and there's wealthy. Walter is the latter, and so are the other seven."

"Who's Jack?"

"Adam invited the big game players to enjoy Fat Tuesday. We'll be heading upstairs soon." Caliste took a sip of his drink, then looked back at the stage, sending a clear message that he was ending the conversation.

A few minutes later, Adam announced with a slight slur to his words, "Gentleman, thanks for coming tonight. We're here to celebrate Mardi Gras in true New Orleans style. Follow Miles. He's leading the way upstairs to the balconies. Let's get this party started."

Everyone moved in a single-file line behind Miles, who stood head and shoulders above the rest. The only way to get upstairs was through Miles office, which was impressively decorated in the same theme as the club. The entire wall behind his desk was made up of shelves filled with vinyl records from floor to ceiling. On a table that matched the desk were two antique record players, and pictures of famous jazz and blues musicians spanning six decades hung on the other three walls.

After they went through a second door, a dimly lit staircase covered with burgundy carpet took them up to a large room decorated with a modern, minimalistic feel. The balconies full of people across the street were visible through giant windows that framed the ornate french doors. Two sets of tall doors opened to the expansive balcony, and waiters stood by each door holding trays of hors d'oeuvres.

Jacob counted fourteen guests in all, including Miles who joined them on the balcony. A massive high-top granite table sat at the center of the balcony, and at either end were huge bowls of beads of all different colors and sizes. More beads filled open boxes under the table. The outside bar stood between the two sets of french doors facing the street, with the bartender busy taking orders from the guests. They carried their drinks and small plates to the seats by the railing, which looked out onto Bourbon Street, the center of Mardi Gras madness.

Jacob ordered a water from the bartender, and drank down two glasses before nursing a third. He watched as the men talked frantically, pointing at the crowd below waiving to the people on the street. One of the guests was trying to throw beads to the people crowding the balconies across the street from them.

Taking in the scene before him, he couldn't ignore the circumstances. Twenty-four hours earlier he had been stranded at a Waffle House with eighty-seven dollars to his name. Now he stood in clothes that cost more than he'd made in the past six months and had $10,000 in cash shoved into his inside coat pocket. He had listened to some great jazz, shared his story with Miss Mabel, and been blessed with one of her meals.

He was still lost about his purpose in this divine chain of events—the *why* still escaped him. He was short for life, death was knocking at the door, but God evidently still had a purpose for him. In his heart and spirit he knew this was no coincidence, certainly not in the chain of events that led to him standing on this balcony. Coincidence was an existentialist term used by nonbelievers as an excuse for God's interaction in their lives.

Jacob walked to the railing. Each man now had a handful of beaded necklaces except Mitchell, who stood by the balcony doors. Most tossed the necklaces down to the street, while a few still tried to reach the balconies across the way. In his life, Jacob had seen a great many things, experiencing the world from the outhouse to the penthouse. He had witnessed greed, gluttony, depravity, debauchery, and perversion throughout his travels, and in many cases ministered to the ones suffering from those afflictions. He knew the stories of Mardi

Gras but believed them to be exaggerated accounts of liquor-induced adventures more imagined than real—until now. What he saw looking over the railing was more than disturbing, worse than any of the stories he'd heard over the years.

The scene below could only be described as sin celebrated. In fact, the goal of Mardi Gras was to purge yourself before Ash Wednesday, the start of Lent. The street was so packed with people that he could only see the ground in glimpses, and what he could see was covered by a shiny rainbow of beads.

Women everywhere were catching beads, lifting their shirts, and yelling at passersby's and the people who stood on the balconies throwing beads. They carried huge containers of alcohol in jugs and tubes in all shapes. A fight broke out between two men, and a woman close by screamed for them to stop. People were passed out against walls and curled up on the street while their friends tried to help them up. Even though the Las Vegas Halloween outreach he'd participated in one year was bad, what he saw below made Las Vegas look like Disneyland.

Shaken by his surroundings, Jacob wished to escape—walk away from what could only be described as the presence of evil. What he saw burned into his memory, the kind of images the devil used as a highlight reel to crack a person's God-centered foundation. The ones that played over and over in the mind, launching a barrage of temptation.

He stood next to Adam and Caliste at the center of the railing, trying to think of an excuse to leave. When he averted his eyes to a place down the street, what he saw shocked him. Walking through the middle of the crowd was a large group of people dressed in red clothing, led by a man carrying a tall white cross.

One of the guests, a middle-aged balding man named Gregory who reminded Jacob of the father from "Honey, I Shrunk the Kids," said, "Here we go again. The Bible thumpers are coming."

Most of the men gave confirmation to Gregory's statement, then returned to their bead tossing—except Adam, who realized Jacob was standing next to him when he turned. Jacob didn't break the stare, finding in his eyes sadness and regret mixed with the blinding numbness of alcohol. Adam knew he shouldn't be there, that what he was doing was wrong. He was wrestling with himself. Jacob could see it. The battle was raging inside of him, spilling out as quickly as the bottle he was drinking. Even so, this wasn't the time to try to reach him. The best course of action was to get him home before things got out of control—and Jacob knew they would.

Adam looked away and walked to the bar for a refill as the large crowd led by the white cross approached. A lady with a bullhorn yelled over the crowd's drunken profanity-filled screaming, "We will pray for you! We are here to help you find salvation. Give your life to Christ. You will find acceptance and love in the Lord. Now is the time. Any one of us will pray with you. Just raise your hand as we pass by."

An odd scene unfolded as they passed. People raised their hands, and members dressed in red stepped out of the group in pairs. Some were together for only a few moments, giving out the literature and returning to the group. Others talked and prayed with people before hurrying to catch up. There was a beauty to it that could only be captured by those who knew God and strove to share his love in a den of sin. It was what Jesus had done—reach out to those who were lost. Following his example, the group dressed in red were making a statement. When it wasn't convenient, when it wasn't comfortable, they were reaching out to the lost.

Adam returned to Jacob's side, his drink filled three fingers high with Irish whiskey.

Jacob continued to watch the group as they journeyed down the street, their red blur fading into the distance. The dedication to their faith impressed him, and reminded him that he needed a reason to get Adam out of the French Quarter and back home. He glanced toward the bar. Miles, Caliste, and Clayton sat together talking, detached from the rest. A new person was doing most of the talking, and going by the pictures in Miles' office, it had to be his father, Lloyd.

Jacob walked over to the men and indicated an open chair. "I don't want to intrude, but do you mind if I have a seat?"

Miles smiled. "Please. My father's reminiscing with us about some of his travels. Dad, this is Jacob, a friend of ours."

Lloyd stuck out his hand. "Pleased to meet you. I was just telling the fellas about spending a month in Paris when we were on tour in 1956."

Jacob slid into the seat and relaxed, listening to Lloyd's tale of playing jazz in Montmartre, while keeping an eye on Adam. Clearly there were two very different groups of people on the balcony—the ones throwing beads and those listening to Lloyd. Caliste, Clayton, and Mitchell—Adam's true friends—were babysitting, doing their best to keep Adam in a safe, controlled environment.

Adam was walking the fence, growing dangerously close to falling off and permanently damaging himself and the people he loved. Jacob had spent a great deal of time as a pastor helping families through the fallout that came when the fence crashed down, splintering lives.

Gregory, the most obnoxious guest by far, screamed down to the street, "Come on up! Hang with us! Free booze, beads, food, and a balcony!"

The others chimed in, and everyone who'd been sitting down got up to see what was happening. Down below was a group of about twenty college-age girls wearing University of California Santa Barbara T-shirts. The men were still yelling to the girls catching the beads and trying to get them to come up to the balcony.

"Not in my house! Those girls aren't coming up here!" Miles yelled.

"I'm coming down to get you all and bring you up!" Gregory called down.

The girls disappeared under the balcony toward the club's front door.

"Those girls aren't welcome in my house! It's not that kind of party!" Miles yelled over the noise of the street. "If you want to hang out with them, you all need to do it elsewhere."

Adam, visibly drunk and slurring his words, moved toward the french doors. "Apparently we've overstayed our welcome. I appreciate your hospitality, Miles, but I guess we'll be leaving."

Caliste turned to Mitchell and Clayton. "Stop them before they even get to Miles' office. Let Gregory know the party's moving elsewhere. They can all grab drinks in the VIP section. We'll be downstairs with everyone else in a minute." As Mitchell and Clayton headed through the door, Caliste yelled to them, "Make sure their IDs are legit. Anyone who doesn't have identification, put back out on the street!"

Clayton gave a nod and disappeared.

Caliste pulled Miles aside. "Sorry, brother. If you could take the men back to the VIP section and get them situated, we'll be out of here with the quickness."

"It's all good. I got this," Miles said. He rounded up the guests. "All right, everyone. Let's join the rest of your group downstairs."

As the guests started filing out the door, Caliste kept Adam and Jacob on the balcony. "I think it's time we call it a night, head home," he said. "It's been a long night. Nothing good can come from us taking this party any farther."

"That's a good idea," Jacob agreed before Adam could respond. "I'm exhausted, and Adam drove most of last night."

"I have guests. That's rude," Adam slurred. "I can't offend these guys."

Caliste held up a hand. "I'm going to make a call over to the casino, have our friend Frank send transportation for them. I'll let him know to take good care of the group at the after-hours club. He can send you the bill. That way everyone is happy and no one's offended."

Adam considered that, then nodded in resignation. "Whatever. Make it happen. I need to call Lizzy and the kids anyway."

"Great. Let's head downstairs. It's probably a good idea to wait on calling Lizzy and the kids until tomorrow though. It's eleven o'clock in Arizona. You don't want to wake them."

"Yeah," Adam mumbled as he walked toward the french doors, "I'll call them first thing in the morning."

Caliste made the call as they descended the steps to the VIP section. There, the room was full of college girls drinking and lounging on the furniture with Adam's guests sprinkled between them. It was a sad picture, men old enough to be their fathers acting like overzealous frat boys caught up in stupidity. Clayton, Mitchell, and Miles stood shaking their heads as they watched from the entryway.

Jacob walked over to them as Caliste accompanied Adam as he said his goodbyes. The only person who seemed to give any pushback about him leaving was Walter Hawthorn, but that didn't last since a petite blonde was vying for his attention.

"This is like something out of a bad movie," Miles said to Clayton. "I haven't seen Adam drink like this in years, not since Jack."

Clayton shook his head. "He definitely isn't himself."

"He's in a battle within, wrestling against himself," Jacob had said before he realized it, and with that said, he figured he might as well continue. "It's a match he can't lose. The only way it ends is if he goes all in for God."

All three men nodded.

"You always welcome in my house and at The Blue Note," Miles told him. "I probably won't see you again any time soon, but I wish you safe travels." He leaned his tall, lanky frame over and gave Jacob a hug.

Mitchell left to get their vehicle and bring it around to the back of the club, and Clayton stayed with Jacob while they waited for Caliste and Adam to finish their goodbyes. A few minutes later, they were all walking through the small kitchen and sliding into the Mercedes van. Mitchell headed in the opposite direction of Bourbon Street, away from the insane congestion.

"Everyone is headed to the casino? Frank's taking care of them?" Adam slurred as he held a glass containing a swallow of whiskey.

"Yes, everything is taken care of," Caliste said with a hint of annoyance.

"Have him send me the bill."

A moment later, Clayton eased the glass from Adam's hand so it wouldn't fall to the floor as he slept.

Jacob looked out the window at the telephone poles and fences passing by, the water marks from Hurricane Katrina still visible after fifteen years, wondering where tomorrow would take him. There were no certainties, but no matter how his story ended, he wanted to fulfill his purpose—and to hear the words, "Well done, good and faithful servant."

Life had interrupted his path like a river carving new ground, but the water of the Spirit flowed through him, and he prayed to embrace its power.

CHAPTER 8

THE KITCHEN TABLE

Everyone was gathered in the kitchen, much like after their arrival the prior day, drinking coffee and eating. The only difference was what Miss Mabel had prepared—eggs, fresh croissants, shrimp, and grits. The conversation was full of laughter, with Miss Mabel keeping them in check as she filled their plates and stomachs.

Adam was last to the table, at nearly ten a.m.

"Now look what the cat done drug into my kitchen," Miss Mabel said. "Looks like you did some wrestling with that fire whiskey of yours last night and it done tore you up."

Everyone laughed more, and Clayton's large frame shook the whole table.

She handed Adam his coffee, then slid a plate piled high in front of him.

Adam pushed it away slightly, trying to get his bearings, then took a small sip of the coffee to buy time. "What time did we get in last night?" he finally asked.

"Right around one thirty this morning," Clayton said. "We left The Blue Note about one, but it took longer than usual since Mitchell avoided the traffic."

He nodded slowly. "The last thing I remember was Gregory yelling at a bunch of college girls on the street."

Miss Mabel spun around at the stove. "He did what? You all better not be acting a fool out there. Shouldn't even be there anyway, that's what I say. Some of you married or got you a serious lady friend. Out there just dancing with temptation, ain't no good reason for it."

Adam looked at Caliste. "Have you heard from Liam? And did my license arrive yet?"

"I spoke with Liam earlier this morning," he said quietly. "Your license arrived about an hour ago, so your all set. Paul asked that you text him when you have time to review your schedule for next week. Liam said that you and the kids are joining them for a barbeque at his house tonight, so he'll get into specifics with you then."

Liam's wife Beth taught at the same elementary school as Lizzy did, and they were like sisters. It would be good to be home and have some time with the family and their friends. It'd been over a week since he'd been home.

Miss Mabel poured more coffee into Adam's cup. "What time you heading home, child?"

He glanced at his watch. "In a few hours. I need to settle a few things here after breakfast, then I'll be taking off."

"Do you need me to book the flight?" Caliste asked.

"No. I'm going to text Paul, have him call ExecuJet to send a plane. I want to get home without any more delays."

They all finished eating amid the normal chatter that came from good food and better friends.

Just as they were about to get up from the table, Jacob said, "I need to thank all of you for being so kind, making me feel welcomed. You've treated me like I belonged from the moment we arrived. It was a blessing to meet each of you."

"It was our pleasure," Adam said. "We've been fortunate to get to know you. I need to wrap up some business with Caliste. Shouldn't take more than twenty minutes. Then if we could sit down, spend some time talking, I'd really appreciate it."

"Sure. I'll keep Miss Mabel company."

———

Adam and Caliste left the kitchen, walked back through the salon and down the hall to the front study. Adam was obviously feeling the impact of last night's drinking, moving slower than usual and then sighing as they took their normal seats in the study. Sunlight filtered in through the shades, casting a line of light across the wall behind them.

Caliste couldn't help but think of a man who'd drawn a line in the sand almost two thousand years earlier. Adam was his friend—his family, really, and he could see the battle raging inside him.

Adam got comfortable in the chair. "What did Liam find out about Jacob?"

Caliste drew a breath. "Are you sure you want to know, or would you rather give him the opportunity to share his life with you on his terms? Maybe just ask him what you want to know, see if he wants your help?"

"What did Liam find out?"

"Well... you were correct. Jacob has stage four cancer. He's terminal. The medical reports give him one to two months, best-case scenario, and possibly just weeks, worst case. The medical data is a bit spotty. He's relied on a lot of different resources. Liam was only able to get a solid record of the past year. He already reached out to one of the best oncologists west of the Mississippi, who happens to be in Scottsdale, Arizona. Jacob has an appointment set for tomorrow with Dr. Atler at nine a.m." Caliste smiled, imagining Adam at a table of physicians playing hold'em for fifty-dollar pots. "Apparently, you will be joining his weekly poker game at some point for one night, in exchange for priority booking. I'm sure they'll be thrilled to see you come and go."

"What else did Liam find out? What happened to him? Cancer didn't leave him broke and stranded at a Waffle House in Florida."

Caliste wanted to argue with Adam, but there was no point in it. He was going to dissect this man's life without his blessing or input. "He had a medical emergency on a plane coming back from Europe. There was a doctor on board who kept him stable until they landed. When he woke up in the hospital, he found out he had cancer and his money was gone, embezzled by his assistant who failed to pay his medical insurance. Jacob's had two relapses, this being the third, and from what Liam can tell, he's refused any additional treatments. It seems he's decided to allow nature to take its course. He became addicted to the pain medications between intermittent care, and lack of resources forced him to buy painkillers on the street. Liam said he did a few months in jail for possession. Since then he's been working in street ministry."

Adam nodded as if he clearly saw the deconstruction of Jacob's life. "No one tried to help him? All the churches across the world that he preached at, and no one stepped up, gave him assistance? That seems insane. There has to be more to the story."

"There is. Liam's working on it. The preliminary information he's been able to acquire leads to Jacob being black-balled by a Bishop Langston. It seems there was an existing issue between the two, the bishop having been his mentor at the beginning of his ministry. I guess they had a falling out a few years before Jacob fell ill, and Bishop Langston used Jacob's illness to exploit his weakness. That's what Liam has so far. I have no doubt when he's finished, we'll have all the details. Remember, this is where things get sticky. Jacob may not know about Bishop Langston being involved at all, so keep that in your pocket for now."

Adam shook his head, his face reddening, then he stood. "I'll talk to Liam about it tonight, but reach back out to him. I want to know every skeleton Bishop Langston has in his closet."

"He told me to tell you he's already on it. He'll fill you in tonight."

"Thanks. I really appreciate your help, especially last night," he said. "I apologize if I did or said anything out of line. If you could send

— 78 —

Jacob in, I'd appreciate it."

Caliste smiled. "No worries, it's all good. I'll text Paul about the plane's arrival time. You can drive yourself to the airport in the Suburban and drop it off at the rental office."

Not long after Caliste left, Jacob showed up in the doorway.

Adam nodded at the chair across from him. "Did you like the shrimp and grits? Most people turn their nose up at the idea of that combination until they taste it. Then they come to understand everything isn't as it appears to be. Sometimes there's a pleasant surprise on the other side of risk. Though when Miss Mabel makes anything, the risk is quickly minimized, replaced with common sense."

Both men laughed.

Jacob sat down. "She's a special lady, an amazing woman of God. You're blessed to have her in your life. I really have no way to thank you for everything you've done for me."

Adam paused, looking for the best angle instead of just being honest. He knew it was never simple, that he often complicated things with his lack of trust. The walls he built were high and thick, made to withstand any attack that would leave him vulnerable. "There is one way you can thank me. Let me help you."

"You've helped me more than you know," he insisted. "If it wasn't for you, I'd still be on the road finding my way to Austin. You've given me what I needed, when I needed it the most. I have no doubt God put you on my path, that we met at a crossroads designed by him. There's no other reasonable explanation. Now, if there's anything I can do to ever help you, it would be my honor."

Adam decided to be direct, no more games. "There is something you can do for me. I know you're sick. I knew in the Waffle House when we first met. The way you ate reminded me of my grandfather when he was close to the end, so I have a pretty good idea what's happening. Fortunately, one of the best oncologists in the United States happens to have a love for the game of poker. I can get you in to see him free of charge, and after you speak with him, how you wish to proceed is up to you. You just have to promise me that money is not a deciding factor. That's taken care of. No need for that to be a concern."

Jacob looked into his eyes. "I don't want to be an inconvenience to you or your family. It would be an intrusion. My illness is not your burden. It's only downhill from this point. My body's going to shut down, and it won't be a pretty picture. I have stage four cancer—terminal."

Adam tried to smile. "It wouldn't be an inconvenience. I have a guest house that would be yours for as long as you want to stay. You meet with Dr. Atler tomorrow, see what he has to say, make your decision after the appointment. If you want to leave, I'll fly you wherever you want to go."

Jacob considered that for a few moments. "Why are you helping me?"

"I believe it's what I'm supposed to do. We both know that our meeting wasn't by chance. I'm suggesting we walk this path together and see where it leads us."

"And what about your wife? Won't she find it odd that you want a dying stranger you picked up at a Waffle House to live in your guest house? I've never been married, but I can't imagine she's going to be happy about the idea. Have you told her anything about me, or are you going to spring it on her when we show up, which can't end well?"

Jacob was right, of course. Lizzy wouldn't take kindly to him not including her when making a major decision. He would be asking her to take a leap of faith with him at a time in their marriage when they were struggling to find balance in their relationship. The problem was he didn't know when to tell her, before they got to Arizona or when he arrived at home with Jacob in tow. But Jacob didn't need to know that. "She'll be fine with it. Hardly anyone ever uses the guest house. You'll never meet a more generous, loving, patient woman of God than Lizzy. Now, if you want to gather your belongings, let's say our goodbyes and be out of here in an hour."

———

Their time in the Big Easy ended just how it started, in Miss Mabel's kitchen sitting around the table. There was something about not just the food but where it was created that led people to congregate. Jacob new he wasn't long for the world, but deep down he hoped to see them all again. They all shook hands and hugged, saying their goodbyes and reminding each other they'd be back together again soon.

Miss Mabel kissed Adam on his cheek, then moved to Jacob. "Stay behind a moment, child," she whispered. "I need a few ticks."

Caliste and Clayton headed for the car, following Adam, while Jacob and Miss Mabel stood at the kitchen door looking out onto the immaculately groomed yard. The sounds of birdsong broke the silence. She looked up at him with tears pooling in her eyes. "The good Lord brought you to us for a purpose. I just wish we had more time. I'd a-liked to known you longer but was blessed to know you at all, child."

Jacob smiled. "In one day's time, I feel like I've known you my whole life."

"He needs you far more than you need him," she said, her tone now more serious. "That child's thinking God sent him to save you from cancer. The truth be, God sent you to pull him out the darkness and into the light. He been slipping. I can feel the storm coming and he fittin' to be in the middle of it. He may never know that this ride y'all' bout to take was all about him. He's believing he going to run the show. That's when that slope get real slippery. Now, child, bend down here, give my cheek a peck, and be on your way. You got work needs done."

Jacob did as he was told, and never looked back until he reached the car door. Then he turned, wanting a photo that captured one of the greatest women he had ever met. He stared at her, developing the image in his mind's eye, committing it forever to his memory.

CHAPTER 9

THREE LITTLE BIRDIES

T he jet landed at Deer Valley Airport just north of the Phoenix city
center. The flight had been uneventful, with both men catching
up on some much-needed sleep. Adam decided not to discuss their
future house guest with Lizzy, opting instead for the element of surprise. It was easier to ask for forgiveness rather than permission. Lizzy
would snap at first, but at least he would be there to explain in person
rather than over the phone. There was some truth in his justification,
but she wasn't going to see it that way.

The door opened to bright sunlight, and both men thanked the
pilot before walking down the steps to the tarmac. Waiting for them
was an airport representative, who quickly checked their identification. Adam then introduced Jacob to Paul, who stood next to the
white Range Rover. As always, his dark hair was parted perfectly to
the side. His jet-black goatee was trimmed to perfection, and dark
eyebrows contrasted with his pale blue eyes. He looked every bit the
part of an executive assistant dressed in the latest Tom Ford.

All three men loaded up, with Paul behind the wheel, Adam

They walked onto the small sitting area outside, then Adam opened the door and signaled for Jacob to enter. The whole room was an open space that was beautifully decorated. Two chairs faced the wall, surrounded by end tables, a coffee table, and small ottomans. Mounted to the wall was a television with a sofa table holding electronics beneath it. A small but full kitchen and a bedroom and full bath completed the house. It was perfect, reminding Jacob of a small cottage he stayed in while visiting Cork, Ireland as a child.

"I had Paul stock your refrigerator," Adam said. "If there's anything else you need, just let me know. There are some additional clothes in the closet, as well as fresh towels under the sink in the bathroom. You're always welcome in the house, but this is your place for as long as you want to stay. Relax, take some time to unpack and familiarize yourself with the place. We'll be leaving for the barbeque around six, and I'll come and get you when everyone is ready. If you need anything before then, either Paul or I will be in the offices above the garage. Try to get some rest." He left, closing the door and leaving no room for conversation.

Jacob stood speechless in the middle of the guest house. It was a far cry from the shelters or one-room efficiencies he called home for the past several years, that was for sure. Most people would probably grab a drink from the fridge, have a seat on the couch, and channel surf, but Jacob knew what he had to do. He removed the Bible from his backpack and took a seat at the kitchen table, then turned to the Gospel of John and began to read.

His mind wandered back to the days when he had a library full of Bibles and commentaries from some of the greatest theologians in history, when he learned Greek and Hebrew so he could dissect the oldest texts, and how he longed for a greater understanding of God. Now he had one Bible. He smiled, thinking of how blessed he was to have a Bible. So many people didn't. Pausing his reading of John to pray, he thanked God for his new friends and a place to live, and for mercy, grace, and guidance for the road ahead. His heart was open, the Holy Spirit alive inside him as he gave thanks to his creator.

After he finished praying, he slid the readers from the top of his head and returned to the Gospel of John. It dealt with the spiritual aspects of Jesus, which set it apart from the other three Gospels, the synoptic texts that dealt more with the life of Jesus. John had always been his favorite New Testament text, Job being his favorite from the Old Testament. And he'd found a better understanding of Job through the challenges he worked so hard to overcome. It had taken years for him to understand that by losing everything, he gained far more than he lost. He finished John, then took his bags back to the bedroom and set them on the floor. Lying down on the bed, he allowed the overwhelming exhaustion to take him away.

———

Paul and Adam were going over the scheduling for the remainder of the month in Adam's office when Lizzy came flying in the room, slamming the door into the wall.

"I'm going to need some time with my husband," she told Paul in a restrained voice.

Adam cringed inside. He didn't know what he could have possibly done wrong, but then remembered there was a stranger in their guest house.

Paul had been halfway to the door before Lizzy could finish her sentence, and Adam didn't say a word. He knew better. Although he couldn't figure out why she was this angry over him bringing someone home.

Lizzy pointed at him with one hand, the other hand resting on her hip. Her eyes blazed. "Don't you say one word until I'm finished. If you want to act like a child, at the very least make sure it doesn't hurt me or this family. I'm tired of you embarrassing me. You don't care about anyone but yourself. You must enjoy hurting me, otherwise I can't imagine why you would disrespect me, our marriage, and your family."

in your position." He waited for Adam to look at him. "I don't have anything to hide. I sat in the kitchen with Miss Mabel and told her my story when you were with Caliste. Anyway, if you want to know something, just ask."

Adam swallowed. "Thanks. I'll do that."

Jacob grinned. "I'm here to talk about anything you want. After all, I'm living in your backyard."

Both men laughed, and Adam got up to refill his glass and get dressed for the evening. "We'll be leaving in about fifteen minutes. Just meet me by the garage."

Jacob watched as Adam went into the house. He then turned his attention to the pool fountains, which shot water into the air above the surface. There was comfort in the monotony of the water and how it behaved exactly as it was designed.

CHAPTER 10

THE BARBEQUE

Jacob pulled the Cadillac Escalade into the wide driveway and parked behind Lizzy's car. Adam had refused to drive after one drink, and Jacob was thankful he didn't have to ask for the keys. The house was in a nice section of downtown Phoenix, in a neighborhood that looked like old money. Large trees, wide roads, and lush, manicured yards. The house was just off Central Avenue, and reminded Jacob of the more affluent established neighborhoods of the Northeast, much different from the landscapes of desert rock that surrounded most Arizona streets.

They got out and walked past the two-story brick colonial to a gate in the six-foot-tall brick fence.

Adam pulled a lever and opened the gate. "If we weren't expected, this house would light up like the Fourth of July. Liam has some of the best security money can buy and some it can't."

They walked around the corner of the house to an expansive backyard patio, outdoor kitchen, and bar area. It was a unique space, with the entertainment area lower than the surrounding yard. A few steps down led to the yard's center piece, a large rectangular diving pool. Behind it were a small pool house, and chairs, recliners, and pool toys scattered everywhere.

A man and two women were sitting around the table, with the ladies talking while the man played with his phone.

He looked up. "Well, look who's here. If it isn't the poker player and The Preacher."

Adam smiled and gave the man a hug, but Jacob, unsure about the introduction, only shook his hand.

"This is Jacob, a friend of mine," Adam introduced.

The two women welcomed him, and their warm dispositions immediately made him feel comfortable. Soon their general questions led to a discussion about love of learning, something Jacob could relate to. The two women were physically different—Lizzy looked to be Italian or at least Mediterranean, with long dark hair and emerald-green eyes, while Beth had red hair and bright blue eyes—but they clearly shared a passion for teaching.

Liam, on the other hand, was not what Jacob expected. His expression never seemed to change, his face void of emotion, which made it impossible to determine his demeanor. Words came from his mouth, but the mannerisms didn't match. Liam was built like a solid rectangle obviously of Scottish or Irish descent. He came across as confident, intimidating, and unapproachable.

Then Jacob remembered Adam telling him that people often misunderstood Liam. He had a unique personality, according to Adam, but if there was ever someone you wanted in a fox hole with you, it was Liam.

"Well, Lizzy and I need to head in the house to check on the kids and get started on the sides," Beth said. "Adam, please make sure my husband fully cooks the steaks. Last time he brought them to the table mooing."

Liam shook his head. "One time I undercook the meat—five years ago—and she can't let it go."

Adam laughed. "You know it was raw on the inside. I ate four or five bites in support, but once Beth cut into her steak, that was it."

Liam seemed to try to smile. Once the women were inside, he turned to Adam with a more serious look. "So, when your wife got here, she was pretty angry. Something about a college-girl picture and Lilly finding out about it at school." He glanced at Jacob. "It didn't get better when Beth brought up you bringing a guest for dinner. Apparently, you never told her about picking up a man at a Waffle House in Florida or that you were bringing him home to live in the guest house?"

Adam stared at the table. "The plan was to talk with her when I got home and explain it all in person. I figured it would be an easier conversation with Jacob already occupying the guest house."

By the way the two talked, it was as if Jacob wasn't sitting right across from them.

"Your wife's an angel," Liam said. "If I pulled that with Beth, I'd be sleeping in your guest house. You owe me one. I interrupted them and filled Lizzy in on Jacob. When I explained who he is—where you knew him from and why you were helping him—Lizzy lightened up." He eyed Jacob. "As far as the college-girl picture, you're on your own with that one. I'm not sure what you were thinking when you took a picture with a bunch of college girls. How many times I've told you optics define people's perception of reality. It doesn't matter that you didn't do anything with those girls. You put yourself in a position that leaves you vulnerable to interpretation. I can't believe Mitchell let that happen. He must be slipping."

"This had nothing to do with Mitchell. He was getting the car at the street," Jacob said. "Adam's associates were the ones who pulled the girls off the street. We were trying to get him out of there, and I don't even know when the picture was taken. Caliste was making arrangements for Adam's guests to be transported to the casino and Clayton was checking IDs. None of us saw it. And if Adam hadn't had a couple bottles of Irish whiskey in him, I don't think we'd be having this conversation."

support you desperately needed. I wanted you to know that I've found enough dirt on the coward to bury him. He won't have a church to lead, and I'd be surprised if he has a wife and family that speaks to him when I'm done. No one will want anything to do with the man. He'll be ostracized, an untouchable. The guy disgusts me, and I'd be happy to make it happen if that's what you want."

Jacob smiled. "I know what he did. I've known for years, but I forgave him. I understand your perspective, but please don't do anything on my behalf."

Liam scowled, as if he didn't understand.

"How can I expect to be forgiven for my sins if I'm unable to forgive those who have sinned against me?" Jacob explained. "He'll be forced to deal with his decisions, but how and when is up to God, not me. Do not judge so you will not be judged, as the Good News says."

Liam considered that. "There was a time in Adam's life when he was an immoveable man of faith. I think he's trying to find his way back. Hopefully you can help him with that. And if there's anything you need from me, just ask."

Adam came back outside with a tray, and Liam returned to the grill to load up the plate. He then set the meat on the table as the ladies and kids carried out salads, paper plates, pitchers of lemonade and tea, condiments, and two rolls of paper towels.

For everyone else at the table, enjoying the food and conversation seemed perfectly normal, but for Jacob it was a gift. He hadn't realized how much he missed simple things like this until the last few days. Things people often took for granted, like dinner with friends, enough food to share with people you love, and the comfort of a conscience cleared by God's grace.

Feeling the need to speak, Jacob held his bottle of water up to make a toast. "I want to thank everyone for welcoming me into your home and making me feel so welcomed. May God bless you all with good health, love, and each other."

Everyone raised their glasses, including the kids.

He smiled, making eye contact with each one.

The rest of the evening was rich with laughter, and Jacob engaged but kept it to a minimum, not wanting to overdo it. Instead he recorded in his mind every aspect he could retain, scribing it into his memory. He promised himself that, if given the opportunity to have more moments like these, he wouldn't let them go to waste or pass idly by as anything less than what they were—a gift.

CHAPTER 11

LIAM

Jacob eased the Escalade out of the driveway and onto Central Avenue. They drove north, past what was once the home of Senator John McCain, which still had warning signs posted on the fence. Adam said nothing, and Jacob respected the silence.

It wasn't until they made a turn on Dunlap, heading west toward I-17, that Adam spoke. "Did you enjoy the barbeque? I hope Liam didn't give you any trouble when I was in the house. It seemed like you guys finished up your conversation quick when I came back outside."

Jacob smiled. "He was just giving me a hard time, testing my tolerance. It was all in fun."

"He tests people's resolve if he likes them. If he doesn't like you, he won't even acknowledge your presence. He's definitely loyal. With him it's not even a question I'd ever have to ask myself. And he's brilliant."

"How so?"

"Liam's cover is as a security consultant, which easily explains his access to some of the most powerful people in business, politics, and the media. But the truth is he's one of the best problem solvers in the world."

"Problem solver. So people pay him to solve their problems?"

Adam hesitated as if unsure how to answer. "Well... he's a fixer, although he hates the term. Imagine you're a politician, athlete, movie star, anyone famous. You're worth $200 million, and your wife or husband is having an affair, or worse, extorting you. Not only do they want to take half your money but they plan to blow up your reputation in the media. You have millions in potential income on the line that can be impacted even if what they say isn't true. If you want to protect yourself, Liam is the answer. There was a time when he would take anyone on as a client regardless of the job, but he's now far more selective. The criteria needed to even get a meeting with him is incredibly stringent."

Jacob was now getting the picture. "How does he do it? I mean, your example for instance. How would he solve it?"

"His gift is as a strategist who can see all the angles, find weakness, exploit it, and utilize leverage. Sometimes he has to create a weakness in order to get leverage. Either way, the result is the same. I'm sure you get the idea."

Jacob didn't know what to say. Adam was describing someone with an extraordinary skillset but a questionable moral code. "How do you even get a job like that, and why would anyone want it?"

Adam shrugged. "Money, probably. How he came into the profession, I don't really know. I can tell you that it was Liam who got you an appointment so quickly with Dr. Atler."

Jacob was connecting the dots. "Is there anything he can't make happen?"

He considered that for a few moments. "I doubt it. Back in the day, not long after we met, he was hired to help resolve a divorce situation. Anyway, I'll leave names out, but a famous female singer's father wanted to make sure the divorce went smooth. Her soon-to-be ex-husband wasn't happy with what he got from the prenup and was trying to extort a ridiculous amount of money from her. She apparently had issues with opiates during the marriage, mostly heroin. The father didn't want her dragged through the mud when she was back on her feet doing well. She was making the right decisions for her future, which included divorcing this scumbag. This guy was a predator, and Liam showed me the paper trail. It wasn't his first time."

Adam adjusted his position in his seat. "Anyway, the father wanted it as clean as possible, just wanted a realistic number for the guy to go away quietly. This guy—let's just call him Ben—wasn't budging, so through a friend Liam got involved. Liam showed up at Nobu in Malibu while Ben was having dinner with his friends, and I'm not sure how it happened, but they ended up in a private discussion by the bar. Liam made an offer of $2 million, twice what he would get from the prenup. Ben cursed at him, then threw a drink in Liam's face, trying to look like a tough guy for his friends."

Jacob laughed. "Seriously? Sounds like a scene from a bad eighties movie."

"Dead serious. Liam called me when he got home, asked me to come to his house, and told me the story. I was wondering why, since he'd never discussed his business with me before, and he then went on to tell me this idiot fancied himself a high-stakes poker player. The biggest reason he needed more money in the divorce was to cover his gambling debt. This fool managed to get in over his head to the tune of $1.3 million. The guy who owned his debt was a high-end bookie in Las Vegas named Sam who was also a poker player, but a good one. Liam already had it all worked out in his mind, every detail. The irony is what happened next was exactly as he predicted, every piece fell into place. You can't make this stuff up, but it worked, which is why he does what he does."

Jacob glanced at him. "So Ben really had no money of his own, only what his wife allowed him to spend?"

"Exactly. He was borrowing hundreds of thousands of dollars from serious people, with no income or assets of his own. That was the weak point Liam found that could be exploited, and he figured being a professional poker player, I must have a way of getting in touch with Sam.

He was right, of course. I met Sam through Jack the first time he took me to Vegas. We got along well, running into each other at the tables, having an occasional drink, so setting up a meeting was easy."

Adam looked out the window. "Anyway, long story short, Liam and I flew to Vegas and met Sam at a Cuban-themed cigar bar at Caesars. Liam explained how working together could be mutually beneficial. The idea was for Sam to set up a high stakes game for the following day and invite Ben. There was no way he would turn down the opportunity, especially if Sam was willing to lend him the money to play. Sam loved the idea. He set up the game, and just as Liam had predicted, Ben was all too happy to participate. The game took place in the backroom of a Bailey's, a bar Sam owned just off Connor Street at the south end of the strip. Within five hours of the game starting, Ben had lost another $500,000, raising the total he owed Sam to $1.8 million. That's when Liam walked in the room carrying a suitcase containing $2 million. Liam set the money on the table in front of him, and he agreed to take it. He kept $200,000 for himself—the rest of the money settled his debt—and signed a document stating he'd say nothing about his soon-to-be ex-wife. A few years later, I read online that he died in a car accident. Anyway, Sam was thrilled. He said that he was in our debt and if he could ever return the favor to reach out."

Jacob hoped he would one day get an opportunity to tell Liam that the past doesn't define his future. That forgiveness is free and waiting for him, that he has an open invitation paid for by Jesus. He pulled into the driveway, drove back to the open garage, and parked. "I hope you don't mind, but I'm going to call it an early night. What time do we need to leave for the appointment tomorrow?"

Adam got out of the car and shut the door. "I'll come down and get you around eight. That should give us plenty of time. Do me a favor though. Pray for me, because I'm going to need it when Lizzy gets home." He smiled. "Oh, and don't call it the guest house. Just call it home."

Jacob grinned back. "Thanks. It feels like home. As for the prayers, I suggest you start praying now yourself." He headed down the path to the backyard.

The pool lights illuminated the water a vivid royal blue, and he stared at it for a moment, then looked out past the guest house to the lights in the valley below. It reminded him that he was just a grain of sand, a speck in time—yet Jesus loved him so much he gave his life, the ultimate sacrifice, so that he could live forever. People could believe they were insignificant, but knowing that truth brought all the peace he needed. His significance was in the role God created for him—a role designed to fulfill God's purpose. Once people realized that their creation was to fulfill God's purpose, not their own, it was as though a veil was removed. The film of deception was gone, replaced with a clear view of God at work in their life.

He stepped into the little house, now his home. Tomorrow would bring another doctor attempting to give him a pep talk while advising him that his time was running out. He would offer Jacob something to ease the pain so he would be comfortable. That hadn't ended well before.

As he got into bed, he breathed a special prayer. "Dear Lord, please help Adam hold nothing back. I pray he opens his heart and mind to not only Lizzy but you as well. May this be a moment that glorifies you and repairs their marriage. What you have put together let no man tear apart. In the name of Jesus, I pray, amen."

CHAPTER 12

THE CONVERSATION

Adam sat waiting in the small alcove that Lizzy had made into a reading area in their bedroom. Soon the kids' bedroom doors closed and Lizzy's steps came down the hallway. He reviewed the checklist in his mind: keep a level tone, don't raise your voice, try to use only "I" statements, above all else be honest. She deserved to know what he was thinking, and more importantly, he needed to know how she felt. There would be some fireworks, he was sure of that, but he would stay committed to having a conversation. He would have to focus on his tone since that was the most difficult to control.

Lizzy came into the room, walked to her side of the bed, and kicked off her shoes. After plumping up the pillows, she lay against them and stretched. "Let's get this over with. What is it you want to say to me?"

It was worse than he thought. She didn't even want to talk. Lizzy quiet was scarier than Lizzy angry, and it meant she wanted to be left alone to process things on her own, that she needed time. Adam knew he should leave it alone, but what he had to say wasn't the same old excuses. It couldn't wait.

Careful of his tone, he said, "I know your upset with me, and I deserve that. The choices I've been making haven't taken into account your needs or feelings. I excluded you from decisions and from how I was feeling." He swallowed. "I was scared that... if I let you into my mind, if you knew how I think, I'd lose you forever. Now I realize that if I don't let you in, I'll lose you anyway. You're my best friend—the one I chose to spend my life with, raising our kids and growing old together."

He'd hoped that would be enough to get her talking, but all he got was silence. He gave her a few moments, then determined she had nothing to say. Feeling deflated, he stood and walked toward the bedroom door.

"Come here. Sit next to me." She was crying now.

Adam's heart dropped and nausea flowed through him. She was such a good wife, mother, and friend—and he was the reason for her tears. He went to his side of the bed and sat down beside her.

Lizzy wiped her eyes. "It's been a long time since you were honest with me. How do I know your telling me the truth, not just saying what you think I want to hear?" She drew a breath and exhaled. "I love you, but I'm tired of hearing bits and pieces from other people about you, about us. You don't tell me anything. You think you do, but most of the time the conversation is in your head. I have to take what you tell me, what I hear from other people, and your side of phone calls to figure out what's happening with you. I just can't keep being the last one to know. It's not okay, and I don't deserve to be treated that way."

What she was saying was true, all of it. "I know it's a lot to ask and I'm on shaky ground, but I need you to trust me. I want to change, to be better for you and the kids. What happened today with Lilly can never happen again. I want to be transparent, to tell you everything. It's not going to be easy, but I'm going to change. I just... I can't do it alone. I need your help."

Lizzy took his hand and intertwined their fingers. "Your first step is telling me what caused you to want to change, what happened."

As much as he didn't want to, he needed to tell her. "Something happened in Florida. Unwelcomed memories all came back. Usually I can just put them back where they belong, lock them away, but this time I couldn't. Jack, the Pokerfish situation, my family, basically all the bad choices I've made. The memories were so strong, and then the emotions hit me like a sledgehammer—anger, guilt, shame, pain, rage, regret."

Adam paused to make sure Lizzy wanted him to continue, and she encouraged him with a nod.

"The night before the last day of the tournament, rather than heading back to the hotel, I drove down to St. Augustine. I stopped for a beer at A1 Ale House, tried to relax looking out at the Bridge Alliance. The hope was to get my mind to slow down, the memories to stop. In retrospect. I was lying to myself. My intention was always to drive by their house. For what, I'm not sure."

"Go on," she encouraged when he stopped.

"Maybe I thought it would create some closure, but instead it made things worse. My parents were outside saying goodnight to my brothers and their kids. But I wasn't jealous. It struck me that it was a perfect moment without me in the picture, like it was better for everyone that I wasn't there. Had I been in the picture, like a puzzle book it would have been easy for anyone to pick out who didn't belong. The irony is that I love them all very much but too much destruction lays in the wasteland between us." He glanced at her. "Do I sound like a rambling fool. Do you even want to hear this?"

Lizzy smiled. "More than you can possibly know, but keep going."

Adam relaxed, more at ease because of her reaction. "I drove back to the hotel, sat on the bed, and got the Bible out of the nightstand. For the first time in years, I opened it looking for some guidance. I was desperate to stop the memories for just a moment, but all of them were standing in line to take a turn. The first verse I found was Philippians 4:6: 'Do not be anxious about anything, but in every situation, by prayer and petition, with thanksgiving, present your requests to

God.' I read it over and over, praying for the noise to stop, for rest or silence." He chuckled. "When I woke up the next morning, my head was clear. Then it just so happened that I ran into Jacob at a Waffle House. I think you know where I'm going with this story, but only God knows where it's going to end."

She squeezed his hand. "Adam, it's going to take some time for me to fully trust you again. You've been treating me like a roommate instead of your wife, and there have been times when I was so angry at you for ignoring our family that I thought about leaving. If it wasn't for my faith in God and the support of my friends, I probably would have ended things. I'm telling you this not to make you feel bad but so you understand I've been praying for this moment. God is answering my prayers. It's not going to be easy, but we can do it together with his help."

He nodded. "Hurting you was never my intention. That's the last thing I wanted. I lost track of what's important, but that's going to change." He kissed her hand, then brushed her long hair behind her ear. "I know God's already working in this. It wasn't just the memories. It was also the timing that got my attention. I should have come to my senses and seen things clearly, but I didn't. Subconsciously, the idea was to always keep moving forward. If I stayed busy there was no time to face myself. It's funny how God works, how well he knows us. He needed me to slow down and that's exactly what happened. I've never lost my driver's license before, and not only did I lose it but I ended up at a random Waffle House at the same time as Jacob. I didn't know it was him. He needed to use the restroom and since he wasn't a customer, they were turning him away. I volunteered to buy him a meal so the hostess would give him the key. It was halfway through the meal before I realized who he was."

"Those odds are pretty astronomical. But it all makes sense when you consider that you were struggling and praying for help the night before. One of the God moments that he makes it impossible for anyone reasonable to explain away. There's no feasible explanation as anything other than his will."

"Exactly. But I really didn't process that until later. I felt something leading me, telling me to help him. I remembered what the pull of God felt like, and there was no way I was ignoring it. That's when I offered him a ride to New Orleans and things started to evolve. New Orleans was bad. I couldn't get Jack out of my head. I looked for silence in the bottom of the bottle. I was desperate, but the ramifications certainly woke me up, helped me see things clearly."

She squeezed his hand again. "I'm proud of you for listening to God's call. Now you need to continue to listen to where he takes you. This isn't something you're going to be able to analyze and think your way through. When Liam told me who you brought home, I knew it wasn't an accident. Honestly, I'm excited for the journey—to see where God's taking us. Your waking up seeing things clearly again is an answer to my prayers."

This discussion was going so much better than he'd expected. "I love you. Your support means everything to me."

"Your words are coming from your heart. I can see that, and that's all I want. All I've ever wanted is for you to be open with me." She glanced at the alarm clock on her nightstand. "Five a.m. comes quick, and I still need to get a shower. We can talk more tomorrow."

As she headed for the bathroom, Adam made himself more comfortable on the bed. His wife was so much more than he deserved. He thanked God for Lizzy and prayed for healing in their marriage.

CHAPTER 13

THE GIFT OF KINDNESS

J acob had spent so much time in waiting rooms over the years that he was numb to the experience. This place was fancier, with high-end furniture and paintings, but that didn't change the reality that he was dying. Yet another doctor would be telling him what he already knew. The only difference was this guy had an Ivy League diploma. Adam had been kind enough to get him this appointment, though, so Jacob tried to not be cynical.

Dr. Atler was considered the best. He knew that from his own research. When Jacob was first diagnosed, he wanted the best but quickly found out that was wishful thinking since he was broke and on government assistance. Dr. Atler popped up all over the internet as being at the forefront of experimental treatments, and now he sat in his office. Despite the opportunity, he couldn't help wishing the timing was different. If he'd seen Dr. Atler when he was first diagnosed, maybe things would be different. The only comfort he had came in knowing that God was ultimately in control anyway.

"Do you want me to stay here or go back with you to see the doctor?" Adam's question pulled him out of his thoughts.

Jacob didn't care. "You're welcome to come back. After all, you're paying for the appointment." He let out a little laugh so Adam knew he meant no harm.

Minutes later, the nurse called Jacob's name from the open door that led back to the examination rooms.

Jacob made the walk as he had so many times before, only this time he had a friend by his side. Adam trailed a few paces behind, and gave room while the nurse weighed Jacob and took his vitals. When she left them in the exam room, Jacob sat on the examining table while Adam sat in a chair.

Within two minutes, an athletic-looking man walked in. About six feet tall, he was bald with a goatee and glasses. After shaking Adam's hand, he turned to Jacob. "I've reviewed your medical records in detail, and I concur with the current diagnosis. Now with that said, I don't believe in offering false hope. I agree with your current assessment based only on the information in your records. What I want to do is a full workup to clearly see where we are right now with your cancer's progression. I can't promise you anything, but I can offer closure."

Jacob nodded. This was what he'd expected.

"It's my understanding that you've decided to not seek any additional treatment. Once I've done a full work up, I can give you my professional opinion in terms of recovery. Depending on what I find, there may be some trials available now that weren't previously. Either way, if you decide to let things take their course, you'll have some closure in knowing my assessment."

He glanced at Adam. What Dr. Atler was suggesting would be expensive.

Adam shrugged, seeming to understand. "I don't care how much."

"When do we get started, and how long will it take?"

Dr. Atler smiled, displaying his perfect white teeth. "We get started now, and I should have an assessment by our next appointment, if a week from today fits your schedule. My nurse will give you requisitions for the tests I need done, as well as a list of the facilities where you'll get priority access. Try to get everything you can done today. Some will require fasting. Those you can complete tomorrow. Any questions?"

Wow. He hadn't expected things to get done so quickly. "No. I just really appreciate you fitting me in on such short notice."

"It's my pleasure. And let's hold a positive thought until our next meeting." He shook hands with both men and left.

The nurse came in, gave Jacob all the paperwork he needed, and wished him well.

As they walked to the car, Adam said, "I have some errands to run this afternoon. Are you good with tackling the appointments on your own? If you need me to, I can switch my schedule around, no problem. It's completely up to you."

That didn't seem necessary. "I'll be fine. The nurse said most of these can be done right here in the complex, and the addresses are on the sheets. Do you want me to call when I'm done, so you can come back to pick me up?"

Adam shook his head. "No, I'll just leave the Escalade here with you and have Paul pick me up. I'll see you back at the house."

"Are you sure?" It didn't seem right to take his vehicle away from him.

Adam pointed to the Dunkin' Donuts across the street. "I'm going to take the opportunity to grab a cup of my favorite coffee while I wait for Paul. I'm good."

———

Adam headed across Washington Avenue to the newly remodeled Dunkin' Donuts and ordered an extra-large coffee with cream and a turkey sausage Wake-Up Wrap. Then he sat in a booth waiting for Paul, who he'd texted while standing at the light waiting for the all-clear signal to cross the street. He loved the nostalgia of Dunkin' Do-nuts, remembering how he'd picked out donuts as a kid. Later while in college it was the coffee he fell in love with during study sessions. Where else could two bucks give you an excellent cup of coffee and a place away from the dorms to study?

When Paul pulled up outside, Adam purchased one of the coffee concoctions his assistant loved so much. It was more like a milkshake they called coffee, but everyone had their own thing. He slid into the front seat of the Range Rover and handed over the coffee shake.

"Everything good with Jacob?" Paul asked.

"The doctor's doing a full workup on him. I'm confident that we have the right guy to give us the best answers."

Paul pulled the car out of the lot. "Good. I watched some of his old sermons on YouTube last night. He's an incredible preacher." He glanced over at Adam. "Where we headed, boss?"

"Let's swing by the flower shop on Union Hills, then McDonald's before we stop at Lizzy's school."

Paul raised his eyebrows.

"I know, not the usual. I'm going to surprise Lizzy with flowers, and the kids have been bugging me for a McDonald's lunch at school. They're always telling me how cool it is when parents drop lunch off, how that never happens for them. I thought today I'd change that since I'll be there giving Lizzy flowers to brighten her day."

———

Paul wondered what had gotten into Adam. This definitely wasn't normal behavior. He'd expected to drive Adam to Durant's, his usual lunch place, then run a few errands before heading home. When Adam wasn't on the road, he didn't do much. Most of his time was spent playing golf with Liam, lounging by the pool, watching movies, or reading. He'd once thought Adam wasted too much of his time—until he went on the road with him and watched him play.

That's when he started to understand what it meant to play professional poker for a living. The amount of concentration needed to

him to volunteer at the soccer fields. David wasn't pushy, but he didn't hide his faith, which Adam respected greatly.

The receptionist in the office lobby looked up as he walked in. "Hello. How can I help you, sir?"

"Is David available?"

"He is. Let me make sure he's not on a call." She stood up. "Who may I say is here to see him?"

"Adam Foster."

As she disappeared down a hallway, Adam took a seat. Maybe this wasn't such a good idea after all. Granted, David had once told him that if he ever had questions or wanted to talk, just to let him know, but a lot of people made offers. In his experience, rarely did they ever mean it or expect someone to take them up on it. He stood and started to pace.

Soon the receptionist returned to her desk. "David will be out in just a minute. Can I get you a bottle of water?"

An odd relief flooded him. "No, but thank you."

Within ten minutes, David appeared dressed in soccer shorts and a T-shirt. He was in shape for a man in his sixties, with salt-and-pepper hair and the kind of tan that came from spending years outdoors. "Good to see you, Adam," he greeted him with a genuine smile. "I'm glad you stopped by. Come on back to my office."

David's office was more like a combination of a locker room, an office, and a storage closet. It fit his personality perfectly, with his life displayed on shelves that held photos and mementos. He cleared some jerseys off the chair across from his desk and then took a seat behind it. "So what's up?"

The discomfort returned as Adam tried to figure out how to make his thoughts into words. That wasn't something he did often, and it proved more difficult than he anticipated. He took a breath. "Well... you told me if I ever had questions, to stop by. So here I am."

David nodded. "Let's pray first. Father God, bless this time together. You are an awesome God and we love you. We pray for your wisdom and guidance as we share this time together. May your will be done."

Adam hadn't expected that, but in a way it relaxed him. He felt safe, more comfortable with his surroundings.

"I've got about thirty minutes before our daily huddle, so ask away. God put you here for a reason. How can I help?"

Adam sat forward, rested his elbows on his knees, and gave a brief synopsis of what had transpired over the last week.

David sat listening, his left arm across his body supporting his right elbow so he could rest his chin on his thumb and forefinger. He never interrupted, listening carefully, then smiled when Adam finished. "Isn't God good? When's the last time you read the Word? Sat down on your own, just opened up a Bible?"

Adam thought about that. "Until I opened it out of desperation in my hotel room, probably sixteen years, maybe more. Before that, I read every day, studied everything I could get my hands on pertaining to God."

David nodded. "What's important now is that you get connected with other Christians who support one another. I wish I could tell you it's going to get easier, but it's not. You can't do it alone. Years ago I believed it was just self-discipline—that I could think my way through things, do it on my own." He chuckled. "Boy, was I wrong. I wasn't including God in all my decisions, didn't have the support of other Christians, no accountability or a church I was fully committed too. Sure, I was committed ninety percent to all those things, but it wasn't until I was one hundred percent that I saw real change. I let go of my false sense of control, acknowledged the only one whose really in control is God. It wasn't right away—it took time—but my relationship with my wife, kids, and true friends grew stronger."

Adam considered that. "I guess I can't see how things will fall into place. There are so many variables outside my control. I'm not sure how to start or what to do next?"

"Start by opening your Bible and reading the Word," David advised. "Let it speak to you. Give God control. Come to church with

Lizzy and the kids this Sunday. You won't anticipate how things will come together, but they will. That's God's promise. Put him first and all other things will fall into place."

He made it sound easy, but Adam wasn't too sure about that.

"Don't put too much pressure on yourself. Just take each day one at a time. Listen, we have a men's meeting every Friday morning. Coaches, church members, men from all walks of life. We've been getting together for the past seven years. Why don't you come and bring Jacob with you? Sounds like you both could use the support right now. It's only an hour, and we meet at Randy's Deli & Bagels on Hardem Street at seven thirty. We spend about thirty minutes just talking about sports and life, the second half we get into the Word. It's a good place for you to meet some fellow believers—good guys taking each day as it comes, just like you."

That sounded like something worth checking out. "I'll see what Jacob thinks. And thanks for your time." He stood up and shook David's hand. "You've given me a lot to think about."

"Good. You made a huge step today. I do have one last question. Have you been baptized?"

"My parents had me baptized at their Lutheran church when I was a baby. Lizzy and the kids got baptized here at the church a few years ago, but I was out of town. Missed it but saw the pictures."

"Well, that's something you should pray about. Baptism is an important step, and it's different when you're making the decision for yourself. If you have any questions, we can talk about it." David handed him a business card, then followed him to the lobby. "You know, I saw Jacob preach at Diamond Cathedral. I didn't understand why they called him The Preacher until I saw him command the stage while speaking the Word of God live. No doubt God's brought him into your life for a reason. Don't lose the opportunity to have him minister to you."

Adam thanked him and headed for the parking lot.

"Everything all right?" Paul asked when he got in. "You were in there a while."

Adam grinned. "More than all right. Let's head home. I've got some reading to do before everyone gets home."

Paul pulled the Range Rover onto the road. "Do you need me to stick around after I drop you? I thought I'd use the next few hours to run some errands before I take Lilly to soccer practice."

"Actually, take the rest of the night off. I got soccer practice tonight."

cheese and a large coffee. Jacob ordered a bottle of water and a dry pumpernickel bagel.

As they stood waiting for the food, David finished greeting some other guys and tapped Adam on the back. "I'm really glad you were able to make it. I figured it would be best to just introduce you once everyone was situated. We use the tables outside when the weather's this good."

Outside, five tables had been pushed together to form one long table. Fifteen chairs surrounded it, and some of the guys were already seated and engaged in conversation. Everyone seemed relaxed, and Adam immediately felt more comfortable. When most of the chairs were filled, David said, "Listen up. I want to introduce Adam and Jacob. Adam's a soccer dad. His daughter Lilly plays with the 07s and his son Theo's with the 11s. Jacob is a friend of Adam's who's staying with the family. Let's take a minute to go around the table so everyone can introduce themselves."

Adam was surprised by the group's diversity. There were grandfathers, fathers with young families, singles, college students, empty-nesters, and some recovering after divorce, all meeting once a week to talk about life, gain wisdom, and study the Word of God. While their backgrounds were different, everyone was treated equally. He had no doubt this was also part of God's plan.

As the meeting came to a close, the man leading that week asked for prayer requests.

"I meet with my doctor this morning to find out if modern medicine can do anything to save me from this cancer that is killing me," Jacob said, surprising Adam. He'd been quiet throughout the entire meeting. "If you could pray for a positive outcome, I'd appreciate it."

Shock and sadness crossed the faces at the table, and everyone agreed.

Afterward, Adam and Jacob stuck around for a while to enjoy the general conversation. It was nice to be in a safe accepting place without judgment or egos. As they left, Jacob tried to hand the keys to Adam.

"Go ahead, drive," Adam said. "The truth is I like to drive on road trips, but around town I prefer the passenger seat."

———

Jacob seemed tense on the ride to the appointment, not saying much. Adam kept quiet too, figuring he would talk if he wanted to. Some people got quiet, others chatty in stressful situations. Adam was thankful Jacob wasn't the chatty type.

The receptionist welcomed them back by name, inviting them to have a seat in the waiting area. Jacob looked even more stricken now, and Adam got two bottles of water from the receptionist and handed one to him. "I try not to ask stupid questions, but are you okay?"

Jacob laughed awkwardly. "Even when you know there's nothing that can be done, that it's out of your control, it's still stressful. Your mind can accept things that your brain innately wants to protect you from. Most of the time I'm able to balance it well, but today's more of a struggle. I'm glad we went to the meeting this morning. Did you enjoy it?"

"Definitely. It's like I found something I didn't even know I was looking for. A group of men who have no alternative agenda and are just trying to live life and do their best to follow Christ. How about you?"

Jacob smiled. "I loved it. Hopefully we can attend many more."

The nurse called Jacob's name, and the men took the same walk they had a week earlier. This time Adam knew the results would be definitive.

Instead of an exam room, the nurse showed them into Dr. Atler's office. "Have a seat. Dr. Atler will be into see you shortly."

The office walls were paneled wood, with the mahogany desk matching the walls. Photos of his family and golf mementos that included a picture with Jack Nicklaus were spread around the office. It had a nice masculine but warm feel and was free of clutter.

A few minutes later, Dr. Atler came in. Dressed in a lab coat, golf shirt, and dress slacks, he shook hands with both men and then took a seat behind his desk. "I have all the test results, so let's get to the question at hand. I won't waste time telling you what you already know. You're cancer is terminal. Your physicians were correct in telling you to put your affairs in order. I think if we continue with no treatment, you're looking at a month, maybe two. This of course is an educated guess. Certainly there are factors that can impact the projected timeline."

He stopped as if to give Jacob a chance to say something, but he remained silent.

"Now there is an alternative option, but I would be lying if I told you it would lead to remission. It could buy you more time, but the side effects may not be worth it for you."

"How much time?" Jacob asked.

"A few more months, maybe six at most, but understand there are results on either end of that spectrum. Some have had adverse reactions and the symptoms aren't worth it, and for others the regimen doesn't work. In every case there will be side effects that range in severity."

Adam could guess what Jacob was thinking—probably the same thing he would in that situation. An extra three to six months would be nice, but only if the treatment wasn't too hard on him. Would he be miserable and sick, unable to do anything but lie in a bed waiting to die?

"If you had my diagnosis, with your knowledge and experience, what would you do?"

Dr. Atler hesitated, clearing his throat, then repositioned himself in his chair. "I can't answer that question for you. It's your life and your choice. My job is to help you regardless of what you choose."

"How much time would be spent in the hospital receiving treatment?"

"Twice a week for six to eight hours outpatient for four weeks, then we reevaluate."

"And what kind of side effectives are we talking about?"

"Typically, vomiting, diarrhea, cramps, sweating, nausea, bleeding, loss of appetite, tremors, and dehydration. In severe cases seizures, internal bleeding, and death. Sticking to the typical side effects, the severity is different for each person. Not every symptom occurs."

"So I could very well spend my last two months on earth trying to stay alive rather than living." Jacob glanced at Adam, who was trying his hardest to hide the horror he felt. "I need some time to think and pray before I make a decision. I appreciate you being direct, taking the time to provide me with my options. Can I give you a call on Monday?"

"Absolutely," Dr. Atler said. "It's a tremendously difficult decision. Take your time. If you decide to move forward, we'll get you scheduled to start treatment next week. If you decide against it, I'll give you a prescription for the pain. I know from your records that your opposed to pain medication, but the pain will become unbearable if you don't manage it." He stood. "I'll wait to hear from you on Monday."

Jacob and Adam followed him to the lobby, where he shook their hands again.

In the parking lot, Jacob handed the keys to Adam. "It's been a long day. I don't feel much like driving if that's okay."

Adam couldn't imagine the weight of Dr. Atler's news on him. "Of course. Do you need to pick anything up on the way home?"

"If we could stop at QT, I'd like to grab some Gatorade. Then I just need to get some rest."

"You got it."

While Jacob was in the QT, Adam texted Liam, Caliste, and Lizzy the same message: *Results at doc not what we hoped. Pray for Jacob. He's terminal but may be able to live longer with a new treatment. He's taking the weekend to decide. If not, 1 to 2 months is the most we can hope for.*

Lizzy texted back right away. *We'll give it to God and help Jacob with whatever he needs.*

cousin Zamir. What did he say? I'm assuming that's the source we're getting this information from."

Liam took another sip of his scotch, then shifted in the chair. Taking a drink before he spoke was Liam's tell. It communicated to Adam that whatever he was about to say wasn't good. "The picture was just the beginning. Once it was posted on the net, anyone looking for dirt could have found it. According to Zamir, Alan is sitting on information to use strategically in order to maximize the impact. He isn't telling anyone in his inner circle about the source. Alan's spilling some of the information to his buddies mostly when he's been drinking. Enough for me to take what Zamir has overheard and piece it together."

Adam could tell he was stalling. "Whatever it is, just tell me."

He looked away for a moment. "So far, definitely some of the details on Jack. Probably enough to exploit after they fill in the holes with fabrication and lies. That's one of the biggest issues we'll have to deal with. In the absence of truth, they'll invent their own."

"What else?"

"They know you frequented strip clubs when you were on the road with Jack—after you were married to Lizzy. Alan has receipts with the amounts and dates. Based on a few of the amounts Zamir overheard, it will be difficult for you to explain. I'm sure they'll find a couple strippers who'll talk about what happened or invent a story. Strippers lying is easy to squash, but the receipts are a different story. He plans to blast this in waves all over social media so the story stays a current topic of conversation." Liam shook his head. "It's going to put Lizzy and the kids through the ringer. People are going to be all over the story since you keep a low profile and stay away from the public eye. Many will get sick enjoyment out of seeing you under the microscope. It makes them feel better about their own lives."

Adam analyzed the outcomes from the worst-case scenario to best case and everything in between. Even so, he felt a calmness that whatever happened he would handle head on, honestly. He didn't care about the media or what other players or people thought of him. His primary focus would be on protecting Lizzy and the kids.

"That's all we have for now, but there could be more that comes out of the woodwork. It doesn't even have to be true. It's what Alan is able to sell, and unfortunately he's a good salesman." He looked Liam in the eye. "I know you've run through all the scenarios. What do I do? I won't let Lizzy and the kids be drug through the dirt."

"Honestly, I would teach him a lesson. You have more money and better resources than he does, and we have so much on Alan that we can burn down every part of his life. That's what I would do, burn it all down. Leave him with nothing, alone and wondering where everything went wrong."

Seeing the worst of humanity had hardened Liam. The choices he made in the past, the deals he brokered, required an absence of morals and ethics. He often washed them away with justification and material objects—although he'd changed in the past couple years, becoming far more selective in the jobs he'd accept.

"What exactly do we have on Alan?" Adam asked. "I know about his issues with addiction. He's been to rehab for cocaine and pills twice. I know he's sleeping with his older brother's wife unless that's changed, and that he's spending most of what he makes. What else?"

Liam pulled up the notes on his encrypted phone. "After Jacksonville, he flew to Hong Kong to play in Xin Chia's private game. He did well. Between his winnings in Jacksonville and Hong Kong, he was up $7 million. Things went sideways in Macau. He was card dead after sixteen hours of straight play, and it put him on tilt. He had a bad beat to cap the session, flopped a straight flush, only to get beat by a higher straight flush on the river. It was a ridiculous hand, but in the end, he lost the $7 million plus another $8 million. Derek Lee and Michael Zhao floated him the 8 mil on credit, which is astonishing. Between the new debt of $8 million and what he owes to our friends in Vegas, he's down $22 million that we know about."

Whoa. "How much does he have in assets and cash?"

He decided in that moment that he wouldn't stop until Liam knew he was worthy of forgiveness—that the choice of accepting Christ would wash away the fear and lies. Now what he needed was some guidance, how a Christian should deal with this mess. He could think of no one more qualified than the man living in his guest house. But knowing that Jacob was probably asleep, he texted him. *I have to go out of town tomorrow for an overnight. If you're interested in joining me, I'll be leaving at ten a.m.*

Jacob had some thinking to do as well, and maybe a road trip would help.

CHAPTER 15

PAUL

The next morning, Adam enjoyed breakfast with Lizzy and the kids. He'd forgotten how much he loved being with them, cooking eggs and bacon while the kids drank orange juice at the counter. Afterward, as the kids got dressed, he did something that would have never happened a month earlier. He told Lizzy what was going on with Paul, the information being leaked, and the options Liam suggested. He held nothing back.

Again, her level-headed reaction surprised him. She asked questions, which he answered honestly even when it was uncomfortable. A few times he wanted to lie or omit the truth, but he willed himself to be transparent. He made it clear that things might pop up from his past, but this was the worst of it—unless someone lied or made up a story for their own benefit, which was out of his control. Doubt darkened her eyes when he told her how much money he spent at the strip clubs, but he explained exactly what took place, leaving nothing out.

Lizzy was worried about Paul. After all, she'd helped raise him. They'd watched him grow from a rebellious teenager into a college graduate, and now it sounded like he was in trouble again. She questioned what they'd done wrong, why he didn't come to them for help. The Jack issue she avoided like everyone else in his life, unable to understand the guilt he felt for something that wasn't his fault. In the end Lizzy thanked him for telling her, and the only advice she gave was to seek God's guidance.

Adam had never imagined that sharing everything with her would be easier than not, until that moment. As he watched her carry their dishes to the sink, he realized he couldn't love her any more than he did right then.

Adam said his goodbyes and grabbed his overnight bag from the dining room table. Surprisingly, he found Jacob standing by the garage with a backpack slung over his shoulder. "I'm glad you're joining me."

"I'm looking forward to it."

Adam was grateful to have some company, and this would also give him the opportunity to seek some advice. As well, he hoped this would take Jacob's mind off things and give him a chance to talk if he wanted to.

Adam opened the garage and Jacob followed him inside. They passed the Cadillac Escalade, '67 Camaro Rally Sport SS, and Lizzy's Tahoe, stopping at the '92 Buick Roadmaster.

"We're taking this?" Jacob asked with a smile.

"Yes. Mint condition with only twenty-three thousand miles."

He carefully opened the large passenger door, got in, and placed his backpack on the floor behind Adam's seat. "Given the other vehicles in your garage, I'm assuming there's more to this car than meets the eye," he said as Adam coasted out of the garage. "Where is this lovely Buick taking us exactly?"

Adam laughed. "Sorry, we're headed to Prescott."

"How far is that from Phoenix?"

"About a two-hour drive. I need to make an appearance at the local casino tonight. It's their twelfth annual charity tournament supporting education in Arizona. Lizzy voluntold me to get involved a few years ago to raise awareness. This will be my fifth year helping with check-in, making the rounds, thanking people for their support. Usually Lizzy comes with me, but both Theo and Lilly have a soccer tournament this weekend." Adam pulled out onto the highway. "The charity tournament has been growing in popularity each year. This time they're expecting eight hundred players. It's a three-hundred-dollar buy-in. Half the money goes to charity, the other half to the prize pool. Plus, there are some other side bets people make. Everyone seems to enjoy it."

"That's a nice chunk of change," Jacob said. "Assuming you have eight hundred participants, that's one hundred and twenty thousand dollars." He reached into his backpack and pulled out a Gatorade. "So what's on the agenda? When do you need to be at the charity tournament, and where are we staying?"

"Players can check in between ten and two. Cards are in the air at two, but some players like to be late. They can buy into the tournament until round six, which is at four. I plan to stick around until four or four thirty, then I'll swing by the hotel and pick you up. We're staying at the Jasper, the oldest hotel in town. I have an appointment to look at a horse property at five thirty. After that I thought we would get cleaned up, check out the town, and have dinner. How's that sound?" He hoped it wouldn't be too much for Jacob.

"That sounds good to me. I'll take a look around town. I like checking out the different shops, looking at antiques, learning about local history."

———

Adam pulled the Buick under the hotel's huge red awning, then informed the valet to take the bags but leave the car since he was going to check in and then come right back out. Jacob waited outside, taking in the cool fresh air. Directly across from the hotel was a town square that looked exactly how he would picture small-town American architecture at the beginning of the twentieth century. People

"I'm not sure," Adam said finally. "I can't just ask him to stop. He'll twist it on social media and make me look ridiculous."

"Do you have to participate in this rematch? It seems to me that you're good at managing your money. He's desperate for not only the accolades that come from the rematch, but also the money to keep his lifestyle afloat. If you don't play, he doesn't get paid. That'll have a ripple effect, destroying his persona. It will cost him even more money since he has everything riding on your rematch." Jacob shrugged. "Instead of playing spy games, why not just call him, tell him that if he continues this behavior, you'll pull out of the rematch."

Adam stood and walked to the railing. "If I pull out of the rematch, it'll cost me $5 million to break the contract. I wouldn't be bluffing, but Alan certainly will think it's a bluff. He wouldn't believe I'd be willing to walk away with that much money on the line. His threat will be that if I pull out, he'll release the information on social media. If I can convince him that I'm serious, that I'm willing to walk away, he might still release it after the match out of pure spite. He'll want to gloat if he wins or rage against me if he loses. If I don't play, I lose the money and he'll release the information anyway."

Jacob feared he was right. It was a bad situation all around. "There is a way to take the leverage from Alan, glorify God, and reach some people for Christ. You'd be practicing your faith while standing on your trust in God for everyone to see."

Adam's expression brightened. "How?"

He smiled. "We take away Alan's leverage by utilizing his greatest weapon, social media. You reach out to an established journalist with credibility and offer them an exclusive interview. It has to be someone with a large following who would be anxious for the opportunity. You'd need to accelerate the timeline and conduct the interview as soon as possible."

"I know the perfect person, Chad Sterling. He's an avid poker player with his own network show. He's asked to interview me more times than I can count. I've only granted three interviews over the years because I don't like how they twist my words to suit their agenda. How will that help?"

"You tell him everything that Alan's trying to use against you. If you do that, Alan's leverage disappears. Acknowledge and own your mistakes, address how you've changed, never even mention Alan's name except to say you're looking forward to playing against a strong accomplished opponent. You leave pride at the door, humble yourself for all to see. Let everyone know that Jesus is your Lord and Savior, and how God is working in your heart, changing you as a person. If you do that, viewers will see your honesty and love for the Lord. It could motivate others to do the same in their own lives. And Alan will have nothing to report and you will have nothing to hide."

Adam was quiet for a few minutes. "I'd be embarrassed and ashamed by my past behaviors, exposing myself to the world on live television, but Alan is going to do that anyway. At least this would give me the opportunity to share my testimony—how God's changing me, the impact he's making each day in my life."

"Exactly. Reach out to this guy Chad, get an interview scheduled for as soon as possible. Tell him you want to discuss the upcoming rematch, that he's getting an exclusive. If Alan beats you to the punch, it will look like you were forced to disclose the information."

He nodded. "You're right. And this feels good in my spirit, like it's the right decision. Let's go. I'll call him from the car."

Jacob stood carefully and followed Adam down off the porch into the rain.

As they walked to the car, Adam grasped his shoulder. "I'd like to be baptized. Would you do it?"

Jacob couldn't have grinned brighter. "It would be my honor."

Adam hugged him, and they got into the car.

Jacob suddenly remembered why they were there. "I thought we came out here to look at the property. No one's coming to show it?"

Adam laughed. "Actually, I already bought it for Lizzy. I'm just waiting on it to close. Should have the keys by the end of next week. I can't wait to surprise her. I have a whole thing planned in my head."

It was like watching a bird spread its wings and fly. Much like the birds he watched from the porch, diving from the trees and feeling the draw to what their creator designed them to do. Like all God's creatures, hesitant at first until they began to soar into their purpose. Jacob's only regret was that he wouldn't be by Adam's side as he grew in faith. Instead he would be a fan in the crowd above, cheering as Adam ran his race.

CHAPTER 16

JACK

J acob and Adam settled into the creased, worn burgundy leather booth. Don and Bonnie's Prime Cut reminded Jacob of the old-school steakhouses in New York, Baltimore, and Philly. The only exceptions were the Western art on the walls and the corny restroom signs that read *Cowboy* and *Cowgirl*. The smell of fresh cut flowers and seared meat filled the room. The bar, standing against one wall and with *Saloon* written in the glass, was from the late-1800s. Brass-bottomed stools matched the bar railing, adding a nice touch to the authenticity. The place had a great atmosphere, and Jacob had missed places like this, although not the pricing.

Adam didn't look up from the menu. "What are you in the mood for this evening, my friend? I'm ordering a ten-ounce filet medium plus, Oscar style."

Jacob tried to find an entree that would tantalize his taste buds without making him sick. "I'm going to have the ribeye rare with sautéed mushrooms. There's a good chance my body won't like it, but I think it'll be worth the possible onslaught of explosive diarrhea in a few hours."

Both men laughed, with Adam nearly spitting out the water in his mouth.

"Thank God the hotel suite has private bathrooms in each bedroom," Adam said.

As they waited for their meal, Adam shared how well his conversation with Lizzy had gone when he called her before leaving for dinner. She supported the idea of the interview, despite how difficult it would be for them, thinking it was the right thing to do in order to put everything behind them. She also believed it would be a great learning opportunity for the kids, seeing their father handle a difficult issue like a faithful Christian. It was good to hear joy in Adam's voice.

The server delivered the food to the table. Steaks, asparagus, truffle mac and cheese, and white corn. Jacob bit into the steak, tasting every flavor infused into the meat. Either it was the best steak he had ever eaten, or it had been so long the memory was lost.

When they were well into their meal, slowing from the weight of all the food, Jacob glanced across the table at Adam. "So what's the story with Jack? Whatever happened with him, you seem to blame yourself for the outcome."

Adam took a deep breath. "Jack was a lot of things. I think if you asked him, he would tell you that he was everyone and no one. To me he was a mentor, friend, big brother, and teacher. In the end, someone I was happy to have had in my life, while at the same time I hated the fact that we ever met. He and I, we..." He shook his head. "It's complicated. Maybe I should just start from the beginning."

Jacob held up a hand in invitation. "I'm listening."

Adam relaxed back into his seat and took a sip of his water. "I met Jack when I was twenty-three, at a high-stakes poker game played at his home. Later into our friendship I found out he was the reason I got invited. The game was legendary, still is, although the players change more frequently. I was naïve—there were a lot of players making waves in the poker world at the time—but when I received the invitation, it never dawned on me to examine the reason I was chosen. I was too busy patting myself on the back, seizing the opportunity."

He took another sip. "Anyway, Jack offered mystery, excitement, an entrance into the world of wealth and privilege. He was old money, and his world was intoxicating to me, so when he knocked at my hotel room door, offering the opportunity to experience it, I jumped at the chance. Less than twenty-four hours after meeting him, I was on his private jet bound for Las Vegas. The destination wasn't even known to me until we were in the air. I was flying blind and he knew it. From that moment on, Jack was the teacher and I was his student."

"What was he teaching you?"

"We landed in Vegas and a Phantom Rolls Royce met us on the tarmac. When we arrived at the Everest Hotel and Casino, a host was there to greet us in a private reception area. Then she escorted us to a private villa that was prepared specifically to meet Jack's preferences. Everything was so detailed, precise, down to the contents of the refrigerator and bar. The truly shocking part was that the suite was stocked not just with Jack's preferences but mine as well. It was one thing to inform the host that he had a colleague accompanying him. But to know my preferences after spending less than twenty-four hours with me should have set off warning sirens. But I was caught up in the moment, blinded by the intoxicating pull.

"That's when my education started, a complete immersion into understanding the lifestyle. He taught me that most people purchase items so everyone will recognize their status. At least the status they want people to believe they achieved. Jack taught me that the goal was to own what only a select group of people can recognize. So began my lessons on what true refinement meant. For example, owning a Rolex Presidential Day Date fully dressed in diamonds. People on the Space Station can see the message your sending. Everyone knows it's an expensive watch, even those who aren't into watches. If I put that watch on a table next to the one I wear and gave people the opportunity to choose which is more valuable, less than one percent of one percent would choose mine. Even though mine is far more valuable and difficult to obtain. That's where we started. Jack drug me through every high-end watch and jewelry store in Las Vegas."

He held up his left wrist. "This watch I'm wearing was Jack's. I received it about a week after he died. It was the only item that he was ever satisfied with, and he wore it the entire time I knew him. Paul Newman was the only man I ever heard him say he respected. When I asked him why, he told me that Newman understood that his legacy in film would die as the generations passed, but his charity would be eternal. Looking back, I think he admired Paul Newman because he was the man Jack wished he could be, right down to his relationship with women. Jack used to tell everyone the story of Newman being asked why he didn't run around on his wife. Newman said why would he go out for a hamburger when he had a steak at home. Jack could never wrap his mind around that concept, there always had to be more. The watch and his home were the only two things I ever heard Jack say were enough. When I received the watch in the mail from his attorney, there was a letter folded in the box. It said, 'Hey, Kid. More is never enough.' I wear this watch to remind me of those words."

Adam picked at the remaining truffle mac and cheese on his plate, then glanced around the room. His expression was hard to gauge. Good memories? Bad memories? Both?

Adam looked back to him. "Anyway, we moved from watches, to cars, vacation spots, proper tailors, wine, scotch, art, yachts, seasonal events, and the history of all those categories. It wasn't enough to know the best tailors in the world now. I had to know who they were ten or twenty years ago. I won't lie. It was fun for me. Knowledge is a passion of mine, and all the topics were fascinating. The purpose wasn't to just move in their world. Everyone knew I was an outsider. It was to recognize behavior and mannerisms and fit into the conversations. This would drop their guard even though they knew I wasn't one of them. A few hours into a game, they would forget who I was and my purpose, which was to take as much of their money as possible. And understanding their social cues allowed me to do it in a way that resulted in my being invited back for the next game."

He shrugged. "That was my life for almost five years. A minimum of two weeks a month, sometimes three, on the road with Jack. When we weren't playing poker, our time was spent in the pursuit of *more*. The best Michelin Star restaurants, the most exclusive clubs, the finest of everything that could be obtained wherever we were in the world."

"Was Lizzy in your life then?" Jacob asked.

"Yeah. She was in the first years of teaching when it started. She was invested in her career, so there was an understanding that this was my career, that it required me to be gone a few weeks a month. But when I was home, all the time she wasn't working we spent together. I spared no expense on whatever she wanted, even buying her stuff she didn't ask for or want. To say I was completely consumed with money, the lifestyle, and consumerism would be an understatement."

He shook his head. "It was strange. I was never satisfied. When I was on the road, I missed Lizzy terribly, and when I was home, the road called out to me in my dreams. The deal between Jack and I was simple. He handled all the travel expenses and access to the games. In exchange, he got a thirty percent cut of whatever I made at the games he set up, nothing when I lost. At the time I thought it was fair. Without him I never would have been allowed into the games or even known they existed. After the first year, it became a routine, bouncing between the different games."

After a long pause, Adam sighed. "Then things started to change in the fifth year. We got pregnant with Lilly at the same time Jack seemed to be losing more than he was winning. He was taking more chances, and his game was changing. Instead of using strategy and patience, he started gambling more. Playing cards, I hadn't seen him hold before he started looking more for hammer hands. He left behind his patient methodical style. There were a lot of snap calls, poor reads that rarely happened before. I tried talking to him about it, but

the only course of action available—to accept my choice and change his behavior to avoid tension and buy himself some time."

"What did he need to buy time for?" Jacob asked.

"To figure out a way to sabotage my plan. Originally, it was only going to be a few months, but when I said sever the business relationship, Jack made a desperate move. He showed his hand, immediately jumping back into character. He needed our trips, the games. I wasn't sure why, but I needed to find out. From that point on, everything he did, every choice he made I secretly scrutinized. Before this we frequented strip clubs on the road, but it was more of an after-dinner thought than an objective. The purpose wasn't the trip, it was to make money.

"After London, every trip we took, if we weren't at the table playing poker, he wanted to be in a strip club. This went on for months, up until our last scheduled trip before my break. It was a ridiculous waste of money and it didn't take me long to figure out why it was his main objective. Before, Jack had always respected the fact that when we were in the clubs, lap dances were all I would accept. He couldn't understand my decision to only be with one woman, but he never pushed. But now he tried to manipulate me into cheating on Lizzy. I let him continue to believe he was in control, that I was the naïve kid he met five years earlier. But he had taught me to observe every aspect of human behavior, to look for inconsistencies in a person's choices. The purpose of the teaching was to win at poker, but it helped me in life as well.

"A few days before the last trip, Lizzy and I were on our way to meet Liam and Beth for dinner. I was complaining about being stuck in strip clubs—I never hid that from her—during the upcoming trip, and Lizzy admitted that it really bothered her that I paid to look at naked women. That she went along with it but resented me for not refusing to go. When I asked her why she didn't tell me, her answer was that I should have known better since both of us read the same Bible. That whatever went on in those clubs, it wasn't what God intended for his children. That it was pure temptation, offensive to her and the beliefs she thought we shared. At first, I was furious, but then I calmed down, realizing everything that she said was true. I apologized to her and haven't stepped foot in a club since that day.

"Things thankfully cooled down by the time we got to the restaurant. The reservation was for seven, but we arrived about a half hour early, so we enjoyed a cocktail at the bar to relax while we waited to be seated. Lizzy was talking teacher stuff with Beth, and Liam and I stood at the end of the bar trying to catch the end of a Suns game. Lizzy and Beth had been teaching together for two years so we knew each other pretty well, but I only knew Liam as an executive security specialist. I never asked what that entailed but knew that part of his job was running extensive background checks on people. I asked him how I could go about running a background check on a business associate, and it wasn't hard for him to determine I was talking about Jack. He told me that he'd take care of it and expedite it for me so I'd have the results before I left.

"I assumed the worst and hoped for the best. Sure enough, the night before my trip, Liam called. He told me the background check was finished, then volunteered to give me a ride to the airport to discuss the results. The plan was he'd pick me up at six and we'd grab coffee on the way, leaving plenty of time for me to catch my nine a.m. flight. I was meeting Jack in New Orleans for the quarterly game, then we were scheduled to leave for JFK the following morning. He had some lucrative games lined up for five days straight in the Northeast corridor. He thought we would be back at it after a few months, but I decided that night in London this would be my last trip.

"On the way to the airport, Liam stopped at a popular neighborhood breakfast spot. After the server took our order, he filled me in on Jack's background check. It turned out Jack had been lying, basically stealing from me for years, and he was deeply in debt to not only the banks but private lenders. When he looked at Jack's financials, it was easy to see that if it wasn't for me, he would be more than bankrupt."

That seemed odd. "How could he be broke if he was paying for all your expenses on the road? He should have at least had the thirty percent you were paying him."

"Right. Many nights a few hundred thousand went to Jack, sometimes more. There were nights I lost but only a handful of times when we came home from a trip down. Plus, Jack hadn't been playing well the last year. Most of the trips, he lost a little or broke even. Remember how I said his style of play changed and he started gambling instead of being patient and methodical? That all made sense after Liam was finished filling me in on the details."

Adam smiled awkwardly. "It turned out Jack had nothing of value. His family home in New Orleans belonged to his mother. Miss Mabel and Clayton were permanent staff paid for by her. She was in an assisted living center with end-stage dementia. His trust fund had exhausted four years prior, set up by his father to only last twenty years. When I met him, he was nearing the end of his income stream. Liam told me there were plenty of lucrative job opportunities, but Jack didn't want to be a working man. I wondered how Liam knew that piece of information but didn't ask.

"Then it got worse. Jack had formed a company called AceKing Ltd. about a year after we began working together. I was listed as the primary owner with Jack as a minority partner. He was paying for everything on the road using a company credit card secured with my personal guarantee. On paper I was the majority owner, and there were numerous lines of credit issued with my personal assets as collateral. He had to keep the show going, so he used a portion of his cut from the games to maintain the credit lines, making the bare minimum payments. As the debt grew, he obtained loans at higher interest rates, moving money to give the appearance of liquidity.

"When Liam was telling me this, I could only think of killing him. I have never been that angry in my entire life. I truly believe had Jack been sitting next to me at that table, I would have taken his life using whatever means necessary. All the money spent on frivolous nonsense that I was tired of two years into our partnership, was mine. The strip clubs, restaurants, hotels, entertainment, private flights, and his personal lifestyle apart from our trips were paid by me. The past five years of my life spent away from Lizzy on the road with nothing to show for it. I had a baby on the way, was looking forward to staying home or maybe a different career path, financially set for life, until Liam told me the amount of the total debt.

"He had twenty-six lines of credit totaling approximately $15 million. At the time I only had $13 million in total assets and $7 million was cash. I paid taxes on every dime of income, not wanting any issues that would result in my life being put under a microscope. I didn't play any games with the IRS like a lot of guys, or my net worth would have been almost double.

"Liam explained my options as I stared at the food sitting in front of me, my appetite gone. I was idealistic, believing that all I had to do was explain to the creditors it was fraud. That I had no knowledge of the loans or the existence of AceKing Ltd. Liam explained that the result would be lawsuits, injunctions that would freeze my assets and have me tied up in the courts for years. There were too many witnesses, along with the paper trail documenting us together spending money all over the world. Jack incorporated in the Caymans, and the banks he borrowed from were in multiple countries. I wouldn't even be able to rely on the help of the United States judicial system. Liam was right, of course. I had no choice but to pay or spend millions in legal fees, only to have the banks use their teams of lawyers to drag me through the courts for years.

"I sat down to breakfast a millionaire only to find out I was really $2 million in debt. Liam was concerned about me taking the trip, believing that the Big Easy was a place with a lot of missing bodies. His argument was that if Jack went this far to ensure he maintained his lifestyle, would I be safe confronting him? Especially in a city steeped in a tradition of corruption that his family literally helped build. Desperate men make irrational decisions, he argued.

"According to Liam, Jack was also into his personal bookie for at least a million. The bookie handled all the bets for Jack and most of his wealthy inner circle, so if Jack didn't make good on those markers, his reputation would be destroyed. The news would spread like wildfire through the rooms of high society, leaving him ostracized. Banished from the only world he knew, his family name shuttered forever.

"Liam suggested he go to New Orleans with me, and at that point I was happy to take someone who was on my side, without skin in the game. After some debate I agreed, so long as Liam stayed in the car at Jack's house. I had to end the charade, sever all ties with Jack face-to-face. I hoped by the time we reached New Orleans, the anger would be replaced with prudence.

"Liam respected my silence, probably welcomed it, on the way to the airport. I was thinking of how to start over, get my money back. How to tell Lizzy, and when to tell her. With the baby almost due, I didn't want to upset her. Liam had all the account names and numbers, which would make it much easier. Not having to track them all down would save my accountant time. Then it was a matter of listening to him guide me through the best way to pay the debt. There were factors such as rate of interest, terms, penalties, all of which would require expert guidance. Since there was no way for me to pay it all at once, I would stay home with Lizzy when the baby came, living off credit for the first two months. Then I would hit the road strong on my own, looking for the cash games and tournaments that would make me whole again."

Adam stopped as the server placed the bill between them. He stuck his card into the slot and placed it on the end of the table. "This is what I was thinking about on the way to the airport. Not Jack or the horrific betrayal, but how to get what I lost back as quickly as possible. I think it was probably a defense mechanism. If I could get it all back, it would be like it never happened. The past five years with Jack, the shame I felt for becoming someone I wasn't, could be buried forever. Later the situation would become far worse. Some memories can't be forgotten no matter how hard you try."

"I know what it's like to find out that someone you trusted betrayed you," Jacob said, fighting the increasing nausea. "When you become so hyper-focused that every breath you take is recognized in your conscience. The adrenaline shooting through your body wanting recognition by action. For me it was a hospital room alone when I was diagnosed with cancer. When I found out my assistant and closest friend had stolen everything from me. Worse, he stole my ability to financially fight for survival. All I could think about at first was revenge, but I had to bury the hatred and dig down deep to find forgiveness. Our stories are different, but I can relate."

After a few moments, Adam shook his head slightly as if answering a question he'd asked himself. "Liam had already purchased a ticket on my flight. Somehow, he was able to get a seat across the aisle from mine. While we're sitting in the bar waiting for our flight, I was thinking about how to recoup five years of income. Liam was squaring up the details, booking us hotel rooms for the night. The past five years I had spent so much time at Jack's house in New Orleans, it felt like my second home. Countless hours spent at the kitchen table with Miss Mabel, Clayton, and Caliste. It never dawned on me until Liam was making reservations that I wasn't just losing Jack. I was losing everyone, all the people so dear to me that I called them family. Jack didn't just steal my money. He was taking away some of the people I loved most." Tears formed in the corners of Adam's eyes.

Jacob handed him a napkin and excused himself from the table, desperately needing the restroom. It also wasn't a bad idea to give Adam a short break. Telling a story like his carried with it splintering emotion.

Sweat poured down the back of his neck and soaked through the armpits of his shirt as Jacob walked. The worst part was often the body preparing for what was to come. He was desperate to make it to the stall in time, praying that he could hold off the vomiting until after the diarrhea. Throwing the door open, he found the bathroom empty. Thank God. No time for the seat cover, he dropped his pants to his ankles and sat just in time.

When he was finished, he did his best to pat the sweat from his face, neck, and underarms. His pale, gaunt face made him look like a skeleton wrapped in skin when he looked in the mirror. His eyes were the only thing he recognized, but they had sunk deeper into the dark circles surrounding them.

Weakness threatened to overtake him as he left the bathroom. Dizziness set in as he moved his eyes, watching images catch up. He stopped, closing his eyes and trying to reset himself. Praying for God to help him push through. He waited a few minutes, his hand pressed against the wall for stability, then opened his eyes. The symptoms were still there but manageable, and he let his hand trail against the wall for a sense of stability as he walked back to the table. Once settled back in his seat, the dizziness gradually left.

He focused on Adam again. "Sorry for keeping you so long."

Adam stared at him. "Are you okay? Maybe we need to finish this story later, get you back to the hotel?"

He shook his head. "No, I'm fine. Please finish the story. I'm better off sitting here drinking some water for a while longer. After your story we can go."

Adam seemed reluctant but nodded. "Okay. But tell me if we need to leave."

"Of course."

"I phoned ahead to let Clayton know I wouldn't need to be picked up from the airport. Thankfully the call went to his voicemail, so an explanation wasn't necessary. When we landed, instead of clearing security at our terminal exit, we walked through the airport to a different security check point. Liam had reserved a rental car, and we dropped our bags at the Marriott, then headed for Jack's place. I insisted on confronting Jack alone. If Liam was there, it would only escalate the situation. Miss Mabel and Clayton would be there, so I knew Jack wouldn't make a scene.

"It seemed at the time Liam was being paranoid, overanalyzing the situation. After a lot of debate, he and I came to an agreement.

He'd wait down the street in the rental car, and my cell phone was programmed to call his just by pressing one. Liam dropped me at the street where the driveway began. No one used the front door unless there was a party or for deliveries. I walked down the drive and entered through the back door like always. "I said hello to Miss Mabel and gave her a kiss on the cheek. Then stopped at the bar in the salon, poured myself a few fingers of Redbreast before heading back to Jack's office. The door was shut, but I could hear Jack's voice. I knocked and said, 'Jack, it's me. You on a call?'

"A few seconds later, Jack opened the door still on the phone and motioned for me to have a seat. He was visibly angry and verbally assaulting the person on the other end of the line before stopping mid-sentence. Clearly, the person hung up on him and Jack in a fit of rage through his phone across the room. We both watched it shatter into several pieces against the wall. I wanted to deflate the situation, so I asked, 'I take it the call didn't go well?' Instead of laughing Jack turned to me and made direct eye contact. I could see the rage and hatred in his eyes before he turned away to shut the blinds.

"He took a seat behind his desk and said, 'How long have you known? That was my banker in the Caymans on the phone. Apparently, all my accounts have been frozen.' His tone made me nervous—controlled, void of emotion, and in stark contrast to his outburst moments before. I saw no reason to prolong the inevitable and answered truthfully, 'I found out this morning over breakfast, but my investigator made the discovery yesterday. He had all the accounts frozen, so you can't steal another dime from me. I'm not sure how you have the guts to call them your accounts.'

"Jack laughed more than was necessary, then said, "Your investigator. That's funny. Let me guess. Your friend Liam figured it all out. Although, I would hardly call him an investigator. Do you even know what he does for a living, who he really is? Compared to him, I'm a saint.'

"I cut him off, 'Liam didn't pretend to be my friend, take advantage of my innocence, and steal all my money. So I'd say there's no events. You and Liam are the only two who know everything that happened."

Adam cleared his throat. "Except for Miss Mabel and Clayton, of course. They lived that nightmare alongside me."

CHAPTER 17

THE AFTERMATH

Jacob watched as tears rolled down Adam's face and his hands trembled. Adam had made a huge step in letting the story escape the vault where he'd locked it away in his mind. Jacob understood the devastation caused by suppressed pain. It was the emotional equivalent of cancer consuming a person's freedom.

He grabbed a clean cloth napkin from the empty booth beside them and handed it to him.

Adam wiped his face. "I haven't told that story from beginning to end since the hotel conference room the day after it happened."

"The more you tell the story, the less power it has over you," Jacob said. "This is the first step, the most difficult one, really. It'll get easier with time, but it's important that you forgive him. You won't find peace until you truly find forgiveness in your heart for Jack."

"I did forgive Jack. It's forgiving myself that's been impossible. What happened that day was my fault. Had I given him the opportunity to make things right, he'd still be alive. I gave him no choice, no way out. He obviously had mental issues that were untreated. In

Unable to sleep, he texted Lizzy about what had happened at the restaurant and Jacob's fall. She could do nothing to change the downward slope Jacob was on, but Adam needed to tell her, to voice what was happening. He then placed the phone on the pillow next to him, just in case Lizzy was awake enough to hear his text and return a message. That was wishful thinking. Lizzy would be fast asleep by now, with whatever home improvement show she'd been watching still playing on the television.

Chapter 18

Welcome Home

Adam and Jacob had breakfast before leaving Prescott, and made it home in time for the eleven o'clock service at church. The sermon described how David had refused Saul's armor, knowing that God provided everything he needed to beat Goliath. The same faith that allowed him to kill the lion had carried him in his fight against the Philistine giant. This helped Adam understand that in battle, as in life, having more was not always an advantage. What God provided was sufficient when you placed your faith in him.

On the way back to the house, they all discussed the teaching. Adam really liked that the kids received the same teaching as the adults, just on their own level in the church's children's ministry and youth group. It made talking about the message and answering the kids' questions easier. He was also thankful that the church had golf cart shuttles from the parking lot to the building. Jacob still seemed overly tired, and Adam wasn't sure he would have made it inside otherwise.

When they arrived back at the house, Liam, Beth, and their kids were already there hanging out by the pool. Jacob was too tired for

Adam shifted in his seat. "That can't be good."

"He's definitely the leak, but he didn't give the information to Alan or anyone in his entourage. It's far more complicated than that."

More complicated? "How?"

"He's not in Newport Beach with friends. He's in Vegas. That's where he's been spending most of his time off. He's flown to Vegas twenty-one times in the past three months. Several of the trips are overnight, leaving at seven or eight at night and returning on an early flight the following day." Liam paused to take another sip. "He's betting on mostly sports but has the blackjack bug as well. He maxed out his credit cards and emptied his bank accounts. The casinos wouldn't lend him anymore money, so he went to the bookies on the street. He's so over his head, it's like quicksand. He just keeps sinking. The casinos can't do anything but take his assets, but the street's a different situation entirely, as you know. To make things even worse, he's developed a coke habit. He's an addict looking for a constant rush, chasing the next high. It looks like it's been going on for the past six months. The numbers show a downhill run from the start, and it just keeps getting worse."

Adam definitely hadn't expected that. "How much does he owe? How much to wipe it all clean?"

Liam grimaced. "The credit card debt is about eighty-five thousand. Casino is another forty-five thousand, and he's got about a hundred and fifty thousand on the street. That doesn't include what he emptied out of his bank accounts or the loans he took out against the house and the Range Rover. That's about another two hundred and thirty-five thousand. In total, he's down close to a half of million."

Adam sighed. "Okay. So our only option is to get Paul the help he needs as soon as possible, before things get even worse. I'll make a deal with him. If he completes rehab, works the program, stays accountable after he gets out, I'll resolve the debt. It won't be a freebie. I'll garnish his wages until its paid so he can take ownership, but I won't charge him interest. Now what parasite is extorting him for information?"

"Originally I went to Sam as the cut-out to make the pitch for Alan's brother's stake in the company. He was perfect since no one knows he owes us a favor. It would make sense for Sam to make a move like that given his history. When I found out you were doing the interview, I called Sam and switched things up. He's happy to return the favor since we helped him with the guy from the high-profile divorce situation. Sam's going to buy up all Paul's debt on the street. That way we can avoid any unnecessary complications and stay anonymous. No one's going to question Sam or give him any pushback. Just as a precaution, he's going to make it clear no one lends to Paul but him, so if he starts looking for money on the street again, we'll know. The same guy selling coke to Alan is also Paul's supplier. Apparently, Paul runs his mouth a lot when he's coked out. It didn't take long for the dealer to figure out he could trade coke for information about you and sell it to Alan."

Paul's betrayal hurt. He had put the family in jeopardy instead of coming to Adam for help. What did that say about Adam as a friend and a father figure? He had failed to see the signs, so was he so focused on his own life that he'd ignored Paul completely? Observing people's behavior was what Adam did for a living, yet he missed this—even though in his line of work he was exposed to so many struggling with addiction. "The money's not an issue, but how do we put a stop to the coke dealer?" he asked. "I'm sure there's debt there to keep him coming back with more information and so he can score. How can we deal with that once we get Paul out of rehab? I don't want this bottom-feeder dragging him back in when he's out."

Liam smiled. "This is the direction I assumed you'd want to go. I was in Vegas last night meeting with the dealer who goes by the name Ziggy, real name Herbert Beckerman. He won't be speaking with Paul ever again. That problem's been resolved. Sam's already buying up Paul's debt, so that should be wrapped up in the next few days. I met with the three casino managers who extended him credit. Fortunately, we had dealings in the past, so it was all resolved discreetly.

His accounts are paid in full and closed. His name is flagged so none of the casinos will extend him credit for the next five years. He was running on whatever cash he had last night, so he has no idea what's happening." Liam sat back in his chair, soaking in the moment.

Adam grinned. "Even after all these years, you continue to shock me. I'll transfer the funds to your account for the casino settlements on Monday. The only thing left to do is confront Paul and get him into rehab immediately."

"I've had eyes on him since I left last night, to make sure nothing went sideways. He thinks Lizzy is sick, so he's coming home. Apparently, she needs his help getting Lilly to her game. You, it seems, are stuck in Prescott after you committed to interviewing players at the final table of the charity tournament. The event has gotten big enough for them to stream it online. Lizzy didn't want you to know she was sick because it was too important that you were there to help. Cat's the best on my payroll, and she monitored Paul all the way to the airport. He should be here any minute. I know it was all a lie, but I felt it was necessary considering the circumstances."

Liam had it all under control—just like always. "When he gets here, I'll deal with him. You've done enough already. I owe you one, my friend. Put it in the box with the rest of the collection."

Liam shrugged. "This is what friends do for one another. Except the money for buying out Paul's debt. That you definitely owe me."

Adam laughed, his body releasing the stress that had built up over the past few weeks.

"Listen, just a suggestion, but maybe the best approach is with you and Lizzy. The two of you talking to him, intervening together, may be more impactful. You guys can say your goodbyes as well. No one will be able to visit him for the first two weeks. He has a spot waiting for him at Pleasant Shadows. When you're finished, I can drive him there directly. That way you won't miss Lilly's game."

So he'd even taken care of that. There wasn't much that Liam couldn't fix.

"Just a suggestion when you confront him. It's better that he sees the love you both have for him. Things will go smoother."

Adam had to agree. "Having Lizzy with me should keep him from lashing out with lies or losing control."

A car pulled up the driveway, and Liam stood. "I'll go out and meet him, then have Lizzy bring him up to the office so you all can talk. Beth and the kids are going with you guys to the game, so I'll see you when I get back from taking him to rehab."

———

Paul knew something was up when Liam met him in the driveway.

"Hey, Paul. Thanks for cutting your trip short. The kids are by the pool."

He panicked a little. "Is Lizzy really sick?" Why else would Liam be here?

Liam put his arm around Paul's shoulders and squeezed them together. And then Lizzy turned the corner—looking healthy enough. What was going on? "I thought you were sick," he said.

Lizzy glanced at Liam. "I'll take it from here, thanks. Walk with me, Paul. I need your help with something." She directed them to the garage and Adam's office.

As they walked up the stairs, he caught a glance of the cars in the garage. Adam was back. No doubt, they were on to him. His first thought was to turn around and run. Either way, he was losing the only family he'd ever known. The realization of what he did—the betrayal, the lies—swam through his mind. Shame consumed him, sending his heart rate soaring and sweat trickling down his back.

Lizzy walked through Adam's office door, leaving it open for him to follow. Adam sat behind his desk, and she stopped beside him, resting a hand on his shoulder. "Paul, we love you. You're a special part of our family," she said. "It's time for you to come clean. We know some of what's going on with you. How about you fill us in on the rest?"

Adam said nothing, just staring at him.

Paul didn't know where to begin or what they knew.

"Sit down," she went on. "Tell us the whole story from beginning to end. Stop trying to figure out how to manipulate us or figure out what we know, and just start talking. You've been around Liam your entire adult life. Do you think there's a chance he missed anything?"

Paul sat in the chair in front of the desk and used his sleeve to wipe the perspiration from his forehead. "I'm so sorry. I can't stop myself. I try, but it's too much." The words just flowed out of him. "When I first started, it was fun. Now I can only feel things when I'm high. It's all I can think about. I tried to control it, limit myself, but that only made things worse. I don't know what to do. I messed everything up. I never wanted to hurt you. It didn't even seem real when it happened. Just some old information, no big deal. That's how I justified it. Until I sobered up, then the guilt was too much for me to silence. I tried to drown it with whiskey and coke, but that made it worse. I kept working to get out of the hole, but every bet sent me further in debt."

Paul started sobbing, his words now jumbled as he tried to catch his breath. He covered his face with his hands, trying to stop the uncontrollable waves of sorrow.

Lizzy pulled the other chair around in front of his, then took his hands and held them in hers.

"I'm so sorry. I need help."

"Breathe. Just calm down," Lizzy said softly. "Everything's going to be okay. Just breathe."

———

Adam was speechless, consumed with fear and unable to move as he flashbacked to his last moments with Jack. The gun, Miss Mabel screaming, blood, the sound of a bullet striking bone, the shock and helplessness that he felt. This time it was different. Paul would get the help he needed. This wouldn't end with Paul losing his life both literally and figuratively.

He watched his wife, the love of his life, doing what Jesus would do. Showing compassion, forgiveness, love, and support to a young man who was desperately lost. Lizzy calmed him, but his tears continued to stream down his face as he rocked back and forth in the chair.

Adam stood and walked around the desk, then sat on the edge of it. "I forgive you. What's important now is that you get the help you need. You're a part of this family, and what happened will never change that fact. We'll be here for you for as long as it takes to get yourself healthy again. The debt at the casinos, the bookies, your house, the dealer—all that's been handled. We'll figure out a repayment plan when you come back to work."

Paul looked up at him. "I can come back to work? How can you ever trust me again?"

"I've never stopped trusting you," Adam said. "It's the addiction I don't trust. Plus, this time you're going to communicate with us, tell us when you're struggling. We can't help you if we don't know something's wrong." He helped him stand, and both he and Lizzy hugged Paul.

"Liam is going to drive you to rehab," she said. "We'll be there to see you in two weeks. That's the first day family can visit. Trust in God and accept the fact that your mistakes are no greater than anyone else's. The devil is going to try to tell you you're not worthy of forgiveness, but don't believe his lies. Remember, greater is he who is in you than he who is in the world."

"That's right," Adam agreed. He knew it was true. He'd seen it firsthand in his own life.

CHAPTER 19

THE INTERVIEW

It turned out to be a later night than expected. Lilly won her semifinal game, which meant she played in the championship at six p.m. Then they won the final in overtime, so the parents took all the kids out for dinner to celebrate. By the time they arrived home, it was almost ten o'clock. The film crew would be arriving at between five and six a.m. to set up, and Lizzy wanted to make sure the house was clean before she went to bed. Adam was voluntold to help, and it was after one a.m. when they finally crawled into bed.

The next morning, Adam downed an espresso. He had to give the hardest interview of his life on less than four hours of sleep. Playing for millions at a final table didn't make him nervous, but putting his life under a microscope on national television had him petrified.

When Lizzy came into the kitchen, he poured her a Diet Coke. That was her only real vice. She hated coffee, but Diet Coke ran through her veins.

He walked to the windows and looked out past the pool to the guest house. Jacob, the man once referred to as The Preacher, was helping him change his life—and impacting so many people with his obedience to the call of God. There was a reason they had both ended up in the most unlikely of places at the same time. It wasn't a chance encounter but God's timing.

He couldn't help but think how different things would be had he not stopped at the Waffle House. There would be no interview with Chad. Instead, he would have chosen a different path with Alan—either buying out his brother's half of the business or leaving destruction in his wake as he dismantled Alan's life. He would have accepted the collateral damage as necessary, justifying that it was the result of Alan's choices, not his. He would have eventually lost Lizzy, unaware of how bad things had gotten, and Paul would have been handled in a similar way but void of the love and compassion. Certainly, he would not have involved Lizzy or told her for that matter.

A light came on in the cottage. Through the window he watched as Jacob dressed in a robe, carried a cup of coffee and a bottle of Gatorade outside, and took a seat on the porch. He looked frail even with the bulky robe draped around him. Was it possible that he'd lost more weight in the past twenty-four hours? Or maybe they'd spent so much time together that he'd grown desensitized to Jacob's appearance?

He took his espresso down to the patio. "Mind if I join you?"

Jacob smiled and motioned to the seat beside him, then pointed to his throat. After setting his coffee on the ledge next to him, he drank a considerable amount of Gatorade. He placed it back on the ground, picked up his coffee, and whispered, "Sorry. My voice doesn't want to listen to me first thing in the morning." Then he fell into a wheezing laughter.

Adam sat forward, fearful that Jacob would pass out as he tried to pull air in between the laughs.

Jacob drank more Gatorade. "This provides at least a few minutes of relief. Coffee has always been something I looked forward to first thing in the morning. I saw you all were up late last night. Everything okay?"

Adam had spent so much time discussing himself over the past few days. This conversation needed to be about Jacob. "Everything's good to go. The film crew will be here in about an hour. But I want to talk about you. You've been dealing with your decision all weekend. Have you decided anything?"

Jacob sipped his coffee. "I've decided to let life run its course. It's time to shed the tent of this body, as the apostle Paul might say." He smiled weakly. "There's nothing else to discuss about me. I couldn't have dreamed of such a wonderful last chapter. God may have caused our paths to cross, but you've been obedient to his will ever since. When my end comes, it will be one of the privileges of my life to have known you, your family, and your friends."

Adam had no idea how to respond. This man was dying the way he lived his life, with faith and complete reliance on the will of God. "Is there nothing else you want?" he asked. "Anything I can get for you or do for you?"

Jacob shook his head. "There's nothing I need. You have been so generous with your support and kindness. I will leave this world the way I came into it. Nothing can be taken with you. The wise man realizes the greatest accomplishment is what you leave behind, how you impacted the world for God. Recognizing that it was never about you, always about him and his purpose. The chain reaction that can change people's direction, motivation, intention, and purpose. It's my hope that I left a larger imprint on the world for God than for myself." He paused to catch his breath. "I can tell you that if you put God first , if it's about him, everything else will fall into place. The goal is to think of God as your only audience in everything you do." He chuckled. "Sorry if it sounded like I was preaching at you. Sometimes it just flows and I let it go. The only thing I ask of you is your company. Allow me to be a listening post when you need one."

Adam smiled, thankful for his words. "I'm blessed to have you here. You've already made a tremendous impact on my life. Please tell me whenever you need help. We're all here for you until the end."

Then he realized he hadn't got to hear Jacob's thoughts on the story of Jack. "Now that you know about Jack, maybe you can tell me how to stop myself from focusing on the guilt I feel for my responsibility in his death. Had I handled the situation differently, helped him, forgave his mistakes, things would have ended differently."

Jacob touched his arm. "It's hard to deal with the choices we've made in our lives, especially when we face the unexpected outcomes that impact others. You had no way of knowing Jack would become violent or suicidal. You have to forgive yourself as Christ forgives us. After what he did on the cross—the sacrifice he chose to make for your sins—to not forgive yourself as a Christian is a sin. Any role you think you played in the chain of events leading to Jack's death is forgiven. Now is the time to forgive yourself and move forward."

Adam nodded slowly. "Thanks. I hope you know how much I appreciate you, how much we all do." He stood. "I better go get ready. I can see the lights coming up around the corner onto the driveway. When I'm done, I'll fill you in on how things went."

"I look forward to it," Jacob said. "But before you go, let's pray a minute. Dear Lord, please watch over Adam as he proclaims his love for you and your purpose for his life. May you guide his tongue, mind, and thoughts as he answers the questions according to your will. Thank you, Lord, and in Jesus name we pray, amen."

Adam headed back to the house and upstairs to the bedroom. He had just enough time to throw on jeans and a sweatshirt before the doorbell rang. At answering the door, he expected to see a cameraman, a producer, and his assistant. Instead Chad was with them, which was a surprise. He wasn't supposed to arrive for a few more hours.

Once the introductions were done, Lizzy escorted the crew as they began scouting out the best spot for the interview. Chad hung back. "Do you mind if we speak privately? I just need some clarification on a few things."

"Sure. Let's go out front." They walked out onto the front patio, where the light was starting to break through the night. "What's up?"

Chad, a stoic man in his early fifties, adjusted his tortoise-rimmed glasses and tousled blonde hair. "What don't I know? I've been trying to get you to give me an interview for as long as I can remember. You were always incredibly polite in turning me down, but after the tenth time I stopped asking. Now out of the blue you call me and ask for an interview. I don't want to look a gift horse in the mouth, but I'm a journalist. There's more to this story that I don't know, especially with your expedited time frame. I don't want to be blindsided or play the fool, so if you could help me out a little, I'd appreciate it."

"This is about far more than just the rematch of The Hand," Adam said. "Which, if were being honest, has grown to be a far bigger story than it deserves. Enough for them to pay us a large amount of money to go heads-up once again. Only this time they've maneuvered to maximize the return on their investment."

"Then why am I here, if not for publicity leading into the rematch?"

Adam drew a breath. "We've known each other a long time. You've been around the poker world, listening to the whispers and rumors about me. I appreciate that throughout our friendship, you never asked me about any of it. Here's your chance to ask about all of it."

Chad stared at Adam as if he was nuts. "Why? Why now? Why bring up conjecture and rumors that you've ignored for the past ten or fifteen years? People who enjoy spreading rumors aren't going to stop. It makes them feel better about themselves. It doesn't really matter if you set the record straight. They don't want to hear the truth if it doesn't line up with their narrative." He shrugged. "Don't get me wrong, I'll do it. If it was anyone else, I would have shut up at 'ask me about anything.'"

"You can ask me anything," Adam said. "The only thing that's off limits is my kids. Poker... well, I'll leave you to frame the questions, but it's all on the table. You just might be shocked at the answers."

Chad laughed. "I'm already shocked. But if this is what you want, I won't hold back. I have to uphold my integrity as a journalist. Don't expect me to not drill down on the questions the viewers expect me to ask."

"Holding me accountable for the answers is your job. I would hope you'd do that."

The men shook hands and headed back inside the house, Chad to find his crew and Adam to dress for the interview.

Adam didn't dress in his customary sweatshirt, jeans, and Air Force Ones. He got most of what he wanted, but Lizzy insisted on an open-collared dress shirt instead of the sweatshirt. She gave him a nod of approval before they headed downstairs. The stylist—a nice lady named Cynthia—had Adam camera ready in minutes.

At first, they planned on conducting the interview in the living room. Then Chad changed it to the backyard, positioning the camera to capture the pool area in the background. Adam didn't care. He just wanted to get the whole thing over with. This was a difficult step for him, and the butterflies trying to escape his gut were a constant reminder. Once Adam's mic was in position, they sat in chairs set up at a forty-five-degree angle with a table between them and the customary coffee cups, advertising the network, on the table. The crew made some final adjustments with lights and positioning.

"This isn't live, as you know," Chad said. "We'll be broadcasting it tonight. Let me know if you need to stop for a break. Any questions?"

Adam shook his head and gave a corny thumbs up.

Chad launched right in with enthusiasm. "Welcome to the show, Adam. Our viewers are in for a treat this evening. Adam, I know you rarely grant interviews, and I appreciate you taking the time to speak with me this evening."

"It's my pleasure," Adam said. "Thanks for having me." Fortunately, Lizzy looked on from behind the cameras, smiling. It helped relax his nerves.

"That's a good first question. Why have you been notoriously media shy, unwilling to be interviewed on television?"

He had already planned for this question. "It's not about just me. When I decide to include the media in my life, my family is my number one responsibility. Limiting my exposure ensures they have some semblance of privacy. Plus, if I decided to do an interview, it would have to be with the best journalist on television."

Chad ignored the flattery. "Do you feel that by not granting interviews, your privacy has been kept intact? When you don't answer questions or conduct interviews, it leaves people to speculate. Often the result becomes the story, true or otherwise."

"I guess for me, if people choose to believe gossip and rumors, that's their issue. Controlling what people are willing to believe is something I avoid, unless it's at the table. There's a poker lifestyle that some people buy into. I'm not a part of that. For me, it's a job. I clock in and out, and when I'm off work, that's my time."

"Well then, let's talk about some of those rumors that whirl around you, see if we can't put the gossip to rest."

"The irony is, whatever my answers are, there will be people who choose to believe the rumors," Adam said. "The gossip will never rest. This interview will become part of the gossip. My intention is to tell the truth, give people the option to decide what to believe."

Chad didn't acknowledge Adam's comment, instead moving forward with his questions. "There have been rumors swirling around you for years concerning the Pokerfish. Many believe that you bankrupted his business, ruined his marriage, destroyed him financially, all in retaliation for his online comments. Ultimately, he took his own life, jumping from the Commodore Barry Bridge. Many in the poker world believe you were heartless, vindictive, and responsible for his demise. How would you respond to the people that blame you for his death?"

When Adam glanced at Lizzy, her smile was gone, replaced with worry. Any response he made would be considered callous and in bad taste. The man was dead, after all. To tell the truth would trash the character of a man unable to defend himself. "These rumors have been following me around for years. I never chose to set the record straight out of respect for his family. His wife has since remarried and moved on with her life. Therefore, I now feel sharing the truth surrounding those events would be appropriate. I threatened to take civil action against him not for slandering me, but my wife and children. My intention was for him to stop attacking my family. Legal action was the last resort. He continued, even after I spoke with him personally and asked him to leave my family out of his posts. When he refused, I did what was necessary to protect my children by suing him. He continued his assault on my family even after the judge issued an injunction and ultimately ruled against him. When the judgment was awarded, that's when we found out he was bankrupt. His wife had already left him for gambling away the restaurant and their home."

"Why the silence?" Chad asked. "If this is all in fact what happened, why not tell people? Let them know the truth instead of leaving them in the dark?"

"Honestly, I knew the truth. My thought was that it wouldn't matter what I said. People made up their minds about what happened, and most liked the scandal of their version more, as they often do. At the time, I really didn't care what people believed. Like this ridiculous picture of me and four college girls during Mardi Gras. I was at my friend Miles' club, The Blue Note, listening to some of the best jazz on the planet. I made a mistake, drinking too much and taking a picture with four college girls who then posted it on social media. My fault in this was allowing myself to be in any position that could embarrass my wife and family, regardless of the circumstances."

"So, do you care what people believe now?"

"I can tell you with confidence that after our interview, I'll never discuss many of these questions with anyone outside my family again," Adam said. "As far as caring what people believe, I would hope that when they hear the truth, they recognize it. In the times we live in now, it's too easy for the media or people in general to spin the truth to meet their agenda. It's difficult for me to trust anyone with that kind of power, so I've always just steered clear. Now, I trust fully in God as my audience. I'll speak the truth and pray people hear me."

"Let's move on to a different subject. You have an exciting heads-up match against Alan Dushku, The Assassin, coming up in less than a month. It's reported that you have an undisclosed guarantee for your participation. My sources tell me you have the potential of walking away with well over $35 million. This is drawing pay-per-view, which is unheard of in your sport. Why do you think so many people want to see this rematch?"

"I think people see how uniquely different we are in our personalities and style of play. We are polar opposites and we appeal to a large, diverse audience. I think that much money on the line heads-up adds to the excitement. One thing's for sure, it'll be intense and entertaining."

"Where does the fire come from between the two of you?" Chad asked. "Is it just pure competition or would you say its personal?"

Adam laughed. "Oh, it's both. At least it is for me. I would be lying if I said it wasn't personal. If I have to lose, he's the last player on the planet I want beating me. I assume he would say the same, which probably adds to the hype of our rematch."

"And what makes it personal? Just a general dislike for the man or the history of battles between you?"

Adam decided to ease into this answer. "I genuinely dislike how he conducts himself at the table and away from the table. I'm not judging him, that's not what I'm saying. What I'm saying is that I personally find his antics repulsive and unprofessional. The mocking, aggressive, narcissistic, performance-driven theatrics that he creates for attention is often degrading and belittling to other players."

"What do you think he would say about you as a player on and off the table?"

"I don't know. You'll have to ask him that."

"You've been playing poker in high-stakes cash games and some of the biggest tournaments for nearly twenty years. Do you have any regrets, anything you wish could have been done differently?"

Adam feigned thought for a few moments. "Yes, there are things I wish I could change, not only in my poker career but in life. The biggest problem is that if you're willing to change something that's happened, you're accepting that you may lose what you have now. I wouldn't be willing to give up what I have now. I do have regrets, though, some harder for me to let go than others."

"Are you willing to share any of those regrets with our audience?" Chad asked.

Adam was nervous but prepared. Now the moment to not hold back was upon him. He prayed for God to guide his heart, mind, and tongue. "You know, a month ago I would have simply said no comment. A lot has changed over the past weeks. I reunited with a friend who reminded me of who I am as a person and a follower of Christ. I'm now willing to share a few of my mistakes in the hope that it helps someone struggling with guilt or shame." He paused to catch his breath. "My mentor taught me a lot about poker, the lifestyle that I bought into hook, line, and sinker. We spent a lot of time on the road in strip clubs, spending a ridiculous amount of money. I knew it was wrong but justified in my mind that it was no big deal. I've apologized to my wife, asking for her forgiveness as well as my creator's."

"When did you decide to become a Christian?"

Adam smiled. "I've always been a Christian, just a ninety-percenter. The ten percent was what I tried to hold back, knowing in my heart I was living wrong. Unwilling to relinquish a hundred percent control to God as if I had negotiating leverage with the creator of the universe. Which is completely ridiculous when you really think about it."

Chad frowned, suddenly seeming uncomfortable. "Your mentor, I understand, was Jack Broussard, a talented cash player in his own right out of the Big Easy. What do you think was his greatest single piece of advice?"

"That's easy. In the letter I received a few weeks after he died, he told me more is never enough. He was obsessed with wanting more. Nothing was ever enough, and it drove him to spiral out of control. He made choices that he knew were wrong, but his mind wouldn't rest, playing tricks on his logic… right up until the moment that he, in a state of psychosis, held me and two of his trusted friends at gunpoint. He turned the gun on himself and pulled the trigger, ending his life in front of us. He was mentally ill—bipolar disorder—but I didn't find out until well after his death. I still struggle with forgiving myself for not seeing all the warning signs. Hindsight's 20/20. I saw it clearly after he was gone. Not a day goes by that I don't wish I could have done more to help him."

Chad just stared at him for several moments. "One last question. Where do you see your poker career being ten years from now?"

Adam didn't have to think about that answer. "This rematch against Alan may be the last time I play professionally. I plan to spend time with my family, focus on what God's purpose is for my life. Whatever it is, I'm committed to fulfilling it."

They then said their goodbyes for the cameras, including the customary handshake.

When the camera stopped rolling, Lizzy came around and hugged him. "I only took a half-day, so I'm going to head to school and save the substitute," she said in his ear. "I love you."

"I love you too." Adam turned to find Chad staring at him with a confused look on his face.

"I feel like I just met you," he said.

Adam shrugged. "Maybe you just did. Thanks for everything, taking the time to fly out here to film on short notice, making all this happen. I really do appreciate it."

He shook his head. "I'm not sure what my viewers will think of the interview. I can tell you it's not at all what they're expecting. But your honesty moved me. I hope everyone sees you as truly genuine."

Adam walked Chad back to his rental then headed back to the guest house to check on Jacob, replaying the interview in his head. There was nothing he could change now, nor did he want too. A few times his words had surprised even him. Throughout the entire interview he'd felt at peace, with the knowledge that God honors the truth. He had been transparent, though he'd expected to feel relief and not the happiness that welled within him. He had told the truth, and people could choose to believe whatever they wanted.

Now he just needed to figure out God's purpose for his life. The fact that he hadn't asked himself the question for so long reminded him just how much he'd drifted off course.

Adam knocked at the door and could see Jacob through the window waving for him to enter. He was sitting in his usual seat at the kitchen table, his coffee and Gatorade with in reaching distance.

Jacob smiled when he joined him. "So how did it go? Don't give away too much. I plan on watching it."

Adam laughed. "It went well. I answered all Chad's questions truthfully. I didn't hold back and was honest about my faith."

Jacob took a sip of his drink. "That's all you can do. Be honest about who you are as a Christian, and people will see the truth. You should be proud of yourself. I know that couldn't have been easy."

Adam changed the subject. "I've been meaning to ask you. When we met, you were on your way to Austin to say goodbye to a friend, but you never made it. Do you still want to see him? We can make arrangements to make that happen."

"Actually, the friend I was saying goodbye to was me. Austin's the place I'd chosen to leave this world. It was the closest thing to home for me, until I met your family and friends. I was set to die alone, but God had a different plan and I'm incredibly grateful."

Adam smiled. "Having you here with us is a gift, and we're all blessed to have you as a part of our family."

Jacob looked down for a few moments, then met his gaze. "When we were driving to New Orleans, discussing your family was clearly off limits. Obviously, your relationship with them still affects you greatly. But until you apologize for your role in the events that led to the estrangement, you'll struggle with it."

Adam knew he was right. Ignoring it wasn't the answer. "There are so many emotions. I'm not sure what to say or how to reach out so I come across as genuine. The truth is they aren't going to believe anything I have to say, so why try? What's the point? Deep down I'm scared it will cause me to backslide into who I was before, and that can't ever happen."

Jacob gripped his arm, shaking his head. "No, you misunderstand. Your apology may result in continued estrangement or a reunion of some kind, but that's a secondary consequence of your primary objective. Your primary objective is to provide an apology from the heart. You can't control their reaction. But you can make the first step and leave the results in God's hands."

Adam considered that. "But where do I start so they understand I have no agenda—that my intentions are pure, and I only want them to know I'm truly sorry? That I want nothing from them."

"Write a letter, express your regret and sorrow, tell them how incredibly sorry you are for the role you played in fracturing the relationship. Don't try to justify or manipulate with your words, just let the Lord guide your hand and thoughts. That avoids unnecessary confrontation and you're forgetting most of what you want to say. Life is a gift. Don't wait too long and lose the opportunity. Say what needs to be said now."

Adam nodded. "A letter would also send a clear statement that the apology is my only motive. Tonight, after Lizzy goes to bed, I'll pray for wisdom and guidance, then write the letter. I hope they see the truth and honesty in my words." When he looked at Jacob he could see the exhaustion on his face. "I'm going to head back to the office. I have some catching up to do. Why don't you get some rest?"

Jacob nodded. "I think I'll do that."

CHAPTER 20

THE REACTION

Three days after the interview, everyone gathered for dinner at the Fosters' house. Typically, Thursday night had become their date night, but tonight was a special occasion. Jacob was going to baptize Adam in their pool. At first, he'd planned to have Lizzy and the kids there as witnesses, but Lizzy convinced him to make it a celebration. About sixty guests came, including family, friends, and the men from the Friday Bible study group.

The guests were starting to arrive, and everything was set up on the back porch. Part of the deal was to allow Adam to hire a caterer. Nothing fancy, but he wanted Lizzy to relax for the evening. She had been thrust into the spotlight for the past few days since his interview blew up the internet, becoming the most viewed episode of *The Chad Sterling Show*.

Adam could hardly believe it. People were discussing it on all the social media platforms, almost all of it positive. He was getting dozens of interview requests and invitations to speak at different events all over the world. His interview had gone global not over the rematch with Alan, but because he openly acknowledged his mistakes, failures, and regrets. Above all else he had proudly stated his belief in Jesus Christ. He had been honest, and people respected his genuine vulnerability and passion for the things of God.

He glanced at Jacob, who sat on the cottage's porch with him, sipping his coffee while a Gatorade sat on the ground by his chair. He still had the light in his eyes. His physical body was betraying him, but his spirit was growing stronger. "Did you know your advice to give the interview resulted in ripples all over the world?"

Jacob smiled, holding his throat so he wouldn't laugh. "I know, but an idea without action is only smoke without the fire. You lit the fire, and that takes courage and belief in something greater than yourself. I watched that interview. Even if I didn't know you, I would have realized that you'd opened your heart to God. You see, a truth that pure can only come from you when God is the conductor."

"I'm still not sure what to do about all the interviews and invitations."

Jacob put the coffee on the ledge, then took a pull from the Gatorade before placing it back on the ground. He was so careful, awkwardly holding the bottle with both hands as if unsure of his strength. Adam could hardly see legs beneath the blanket covering Jacob's lap. "You already know what you're supposed to do. Allow God to be your shepherd. Follow where his purpose takes you. If it's about you, it's not about him. That's one of the easiest tests when making a decision. Ask yourself honestly if this is about glorifying God or my own agenda. You'll get a quick answer, I promise you. There will be times where you make the mistake of justification to obtain what you want instead of what you need. You'll know when that happens. We all make that mistake. After all, we're human. The only person who was perfect died a horrible death when he didn't have to, for all of humanity."

When Adam glanced toward the house, people were starting to arrive. Some of the guys from the men's group had come with their families. He should greet them, but he wanted to stay and talk with Jacob, knowing he had few of these moments left.

"Go on up and greet your guests," Jacob said as if reading his mind. "I'll hang out down here until the baptism. I'm only walking up those stairs one time a day." He smiled, then braced himself to get up from the chair.

Adam took his arm and helped him to his feet.

"I knew the downward slope was coming, but I thought there'd be a break along the way. I'm going to head into the house and rest a bit until its time."

As he did that, Adam walked back up the lawn and climbed the steps to meet his guests. Almost everyone from the men's group was there, and even those who'd had to work had sent texts congratulating him.

David introduced his wife, then asked, "How's Jacob feeling?"

Adam turned him away from the crowd to minimize the noise. "He's weak. When we visit, its usually down by the pool. The stairs are difficult for him, so he only comes up to the house for dinner. He's down getting some rest before the baptism."

"I talked to the guys, and we want to make sure Jacob gets to men's group for prayers and encouragement," David said. "I know he's really struggling, so how would you feel about us all meeting here tomorrow morning? That way he can be a part of it. We'll meet here for as long as he'd like, if that's cool with you."

Adam hadn't thought of that, but it was a great idea. "Sure."

"Great. I can pick up bagels on the way since I pass by Randy's. If you have coffee and hot tea, then were good."

"That would be awesome. I really appreciate it, and I know he will too."

Adam took a double take when Liam arrived late with Beth and the kids. Liam had texted earlier in the day to apologize for missing the baptism.

"It appears my hypocrisy knows no bounds," he said, quoting Doc Holiday in *Tombstone*, when Adam greeted him.

He laughed. That was a running joke between them, but in this case, there was an underlying meaning to the statement. "Thanks for coming. It means a lot."

Lizzy announced that they would be starting in five minutes, and the guests began to make their way poolside. As soon as everyone was settled, Jacob led them in prayer and then read Scripture to outline the meaning of baptism. Surprisingly, he also invited anyone to come forward who wished to be baptized.

Jacob moved slowly into the water, using the railing to take each step carefully. David quickly took off his shoes and socks, then moved to the steps and assisted Adam with Jacob, helping the remainder of the way. Jacob prayed again, then asked Adam if he wished to be baptized.

"Yes, there is nothing I want more than to know God and fulfill his purpose for my life," he answered.

"I baptize you in the name of the Father, and of the Son, and of the Holy Spirit." With David's help, he submerged Adam into the water.

When Adam came up, everyone was cheering and praising God. The gratitude he felt for what Jesus had done on the cross overwhelmed him. It was a freedom he had never experienced, a peace that was all consuming.

He and David then helped Jacob up the pool stairs and straight into the guest house. Jacob was shaking from the cold, and it was important to get him warm quickly. The two guided him to the bedroom and carefully helped him into dry clothes.

"Thanks. I didn't realize how cold the water was," Jacob said. "I'd like to rest a bit, then I'll be up. That took more out of me than I thought it would."

David wrapped Jacob's blanket around his shoulders. "How about we come back to check on you in twenty minutes?"

Jacob nodded and let them help him under the covers.

David shook his head when he and Adam stepped out onto the porch. "He's gone downhill so quickly. Only a week ago he was okay mobility wise."

"Yeah. When I mentioned that to Dr. Atler, he told me this isn't uncommon, especially in Jacob's case. He gave me the number for the best twenty-four-hour nursing care available. I'm going to call and get someone here tonight to help him."

Adam acknowledged his guests, engaging in general conversation and thanked them for coming. He then pulled Lizzy aside to let her know how poorly Jacob was doing and headed for his office.

Liam caught up to him on the front porch. "Everything okay?"

"Jacob's decompensating quickly. He's resting now, but I'm going up to the office to get the number for the in-home care service Dr. Atler recommended."

Liam stopped. "Do that. I'll go down and make sure he's okay." Then he was gone.

————

Liam headed for the guest house, avoiding anyone who would slow him down. He knocked a few times, then let himself in. He'd expected Jacob to be in the bedroom, but he was sitting at the kitchen table with his Bible opened in front of him and a blanket around his shoulders.

"Adam's taking care of a few things, then he'll be down. Can I get you anything?"

Jacob smiled. "If you could get me some Gatorade from the fridge, that would be great. I've been wondering when we would have some time to talk. It seems God is giving us that opportunity now."

Liam poured the Gatorade into a glass, handed it to him, returned the bottle to the fridge, and sat down at the table. "What is it that you want to talk about?"

Jacob took a drink, using two hands at first and then switching to one. After setting the glass on the table, he said, "When Paul was

Saul, he was struck blind. The Bible says scales fell from his eyes three days later and he could see clearly, believing in the Son of Man. Jesus forced him to rely on the people he was persecuting. You see, Paul was tracking down the early Christians and killing them, whole families. God asked them to show mercy to the man who was hunting them. Paul accepted the words of Jesus as truth, knowing in his heart that Jesus was the Messiah. The Lord gave him time to rely on others for his safety, until God opened his eyes."

Liam knew the story well. He had been raised in church. When he was a child, it had been a place where he found refuge, comfort, and acceptance. "What is it about Paul that made him so special? If he was persecuting Christians, why not wipe him from the earth?"

Jacob smiled again. "That wasn't God's purpose. Instead Paul became a beacon of hope as a shepherd among the gentiles. God used him to pen nearly half the New Testament. Like Paul, God has a purpose for all of us."

Now he understood where the conversation was going. "I've done things, horrible things, that can't be erased. Every day I try to be a better person, but that doesn't undue the past. I hear what you're saying, but there's no way someone like me can be forgiven." Fear settled inside him, something he hadn't felt in years. "I've tried in the past, but something would happen and I'd get pulled back into my old ways. I don't want that for my children. I want them to know Jesus. But for me, I can't see how that would work in my life."

"I promise you that you haven't done worse in your life than Paul," Jacob said. "Understand, though, one sin is no greater than another. Original sin is in all of us. We're all sinners, but Jesus forgives. He made the ultimate sacrifice, atoning for all of our sins with his blood. That's love. *God* is love. So many miss that fundamental truth when they seek him. He loved us so much that he died when he didn't have to so we could live forever with him. I'm no more worthy of his love or death than you or anyone else. The doubt you feel is the devil lying to you, trying to convince you that you're not good enough."

Liam could barely breathe. His chest ached. Resting his elbows on the table, he put his face in his hands. "I don't know how."

Jacob squeezed his arm. "You don't have to. You just have to trust him. If you believe Jesus is your Lord and Savior, accept him into your heart. He is the way, the truth, and the light. Whosoever believes in him shall never perish but have everlasting life. That's his word, his promise to us all. You're not alone in your walk. Everyone is here to support you."

The anxiety only seemed to swell inside him. Questions rushed through his mind. How would he do his job? What about the relationships he'd built? The choice to follow Jesus would impact his life. Could he handle that?

Suddenly a Scripture verse from years before came to mind—the first verse he'd ever memorized: *Greater is he who is in you, than he who is in the world.*

When Liam looked up, he saw understanding and compassion in Jacob's hollowed eyes. The man was dying but still taking the time to remind him of what he'd always known, before being blinded by the world. "What do I need to do to accept Jesus? I know I have to pray to him, but what exactly do I say?"

"Repeat this prayer after me, acknowledging Jesus as your Lord and Savior."

They closed their eyes and bowed their heads, and Jacob recited the salvation prayer with Liam repeating his words. When they finished, they opened their eyes to find Adam and David standing just inside the door.

Liam quickly wiped his eyes. "How long you been standing there?"

"Long enough. I couldn't be happier for you. We'll be in this together, my friend, holding each other accountable."

It had been years since Liam had felt free. An awkward sense of peace replaced the chaos that had filled his mind. It would take work and commitment to grow in his faith, but he would do it.

Jacob braced his hands against the table to stand up. "Now we just have to baptize you," he told Liam.

Liam hadn't considered that. He looked at Adam. "This is your day. I'll get baptized some other time. I still have to tell Beth what happened, and I'll probably need you there to confirm that it's not a joke."

Everyone laughed.

"This isn't my day," Adam insisted. "This is God's day. Now it's yours as well. Why don't you go tell Beth that you're getting baptized?"

Things were moving fast, and Liam hated the feeling of losing control. It was something he rarely experienced, although he realized he'd need to get used to it, acknowledging God was running the show.

"I'd like to be a part of the baptism, but I can't get in the water again," Jacob said. "If I do the speaking, will you two go in the water?"

Both David and Adam agreed, and Adam suggested he go tell Beth.

Liam couldn't wait to see the look on her face.

———

While Liam went in search of Beth, David and Adam picked up Jacob's chair and carried it outside to the pool. Lizzy's announcement could probably be heard two counties over, and everyone moved back down from the porch and gathered once again around the shallow end of the pool.

Jacob performed the ceremony again, only this time with new Scripture verses. David and Adam stood in the pool next to Liam, and Beth and the kids watched from the pool's edge as their family became whole. She smiled and cried, her expression one of absolute joy.

When Liam's baptism was finished, they returned Jacob to his kitchen. He made a joke along the way that his mind was still sharp and it was his body that betrayed him. Then David spent time talking to Liam while Adam fulfilled his host responsibilities.

When the party ended, Liam and Beth stayed behind to help clean up. It was the least enjoyable part of having company, but when Adam looked around, he saw family. Liam and Beth had done life with him and Lizzy for a long time. It wasn't just the quantity of time but rather the shared experiences that intertwined their history. Although he missed his parents and family, he had people who loved and cared about him. They were family bound not by blood but God's purpose, committed to caring for one another in the worst and best of times. There was no agenda, just the freedom to live without judgment or justification.

Afterward, Adam and Liam went to check on Jacob. "So, Mr. Poker Player, I bet you didn't see that one coming," Liam said as they walked off the porch.

Adam laughed. "Definitely not. What changed your mind so quickly?"

He pointed at the guest house. "That guy. Honestly, researching him put me outside my box. How he forgave Bishop Langston after what he did, I couldn't stop thinking about it. Listening to him on YouTube, what he said and how he said it, I found myself wanting to hear more, then I started asking myself some hard questions. I know it seems like a quick decision, but it really wasn't. I've felt something building inside me, and when I sat with Jacob tonight, I could feel the dam start to crack. I'm probably not making any sense. It's hard to explain."

But Adam did understand. "Actually, it's crystal clear to me. I know exactly what you mean." He knocked at the door, not wanting to walk in and startle the nurse who'd arrived an hour earlier. Sadie looked to be in her early fifties, was built like a spark plug, and had a no-nonsense attitude to match. Adam liked her immediately, having always gravitated toward people who were direct. People like that were usually honest and didn't spend a lot of time thinking about how to say something. They didn't have a filter, so it was brain to mouth, without enough time to say anything other than the truth.

Sadie answered the door and let them in despite the frustration on her face. "Now I just got him settled in the bedroom. You can go on in, but keep it short. He needs his rest."

"Absolutely," Adam said. Once they were in the room, he asked, "How you feeling? Miss Sadie have you squared away?"

Jacob mouthed the word *sergeant* and gave a salute, then smiled. "I'm doing well. She really is a help. Thanks for bringing her here."

Adam waved that away. "We just wanted to say goodnight before Liam takes off, make sure you're good to go. Also, the guys will be meeting here on Friday mornings, so you'll see everyone tomorrow. Liam's going to be joining us as well."

"I am?" Liam said. "What time is men's group?"

Adam grinned. Liam hated waking up early. "We start promptly at seven thirty, so you should be able to sleep in until about six thirty, six forty-five."

He rolled his eyes. "I'll be here, but I don't know why you guys chose to meet at the crack of dawn. God's awake all the time, isn't he? Is there a reason we can't meet at a normal time?" When neither Adam nor Jacob responded, he grinned. "Whatever. I'll be here." He looked at Jacob. "Thank you for everything today, It meant a lot to my family and me."

Jacob gave a nod of understanding and mouthed *good night*.

As the two men walked back to the house, Liam asked, "Is there anything he needs that Beth and I can provide?"

"I've asked him a few times and he's told me there's nothing else he wants, says he's content."

Stepping inside, Adam pondered the idea of contentment. From this day on, he would focus on what he had instead of what he didn't.

CHAPTER 21

THE ALPHA

It was Liam's fourth time attending men's group, which was now something he looked forward to all week. So much had changed in the last month. People had told him he'd start to see things differently, but that sounded like just words until he started to live it.

As he pulled into Adam's driveway—early, as usual—Christian music played on the radio. Something he didn't think would happen in a million years. The rest of the men would start arriving in about thirty minutes, but he needed to discuss some business with Adam beforehand.

"Good morning," Liam said as he walked into Adam's office. He headed for the bar, and grinned when Adam's eyes widened. "Just messing with you." He turned and took his usual chair. "I thought your reaction would be priceless and I was right. How was Jacob yesterday?"

"I had to take care of some business, so I only got to see him at the end of the day. He seemed good. Sadie said a few guys from men's group came to visit with him. It's cool guys are stopping by every day.

I think Jacob enjoys it. He can't talk much, but they watch whatever game or cooking show is on—or *Jeopardy*. The man loves *Jeopardy*. Sadie gives me reports throughout the day. Oddly, he does better in the morning and at night, not so good midday. Are we good to go for his surprise?"

"Yeah, it's all set up. I just have to input the link. Sadie won't be happy, but I figure we can forego the wheelchair since he doesn't like it, just pick up his chair like we did for the baptism, and carry him up to the house. That way there's plenty of room for everyone to see. I hope he likes what we've done."

"I'm sure he will, especially since he knows that it's coming from the heart. I was thinking. You severed ties with Alan's cousin, right? We settled what was owed, you let him know we won't be calling again?"

Liam pulled his phone from his pocket to quiet its buzzing. "Yeah, the day after your interview aired. Why do you ask?"

Adam got up and walked to the window. "It's just important moving forward that we both make a commitment to doing things the right way—God's way. Otherwise I want nothing to do with it. Especially now that we're using our knowledge, resources, and experience to make a real impact in the community. The devil's going to look for cracks in our foundation, so we need to make sure there's nowhere he can go."

"I agree. I turned all my clients over to Cat the day after the baptism. She's worked for me a long time, and it's what she always wanted. I'm looking forward to using my skill set in a positive way, to make a difference. The more I look back, the harder it is to forgive myself. That will probably be the hardest step. David told me that over time he was able to stop focusing on his mistakes, that it still happens but not nearly as often as it did in the beginning. He said that as I grow in my faith, I'll understand that not forgiving myself is a sin and that acknowledging that Jesus paid the ultimate sacrifice is accepting the fact that you're forgiven."

Cars pulled up outside, and Liam looked at his watch. Seven twenty-five. They met David in the driveway and walked down to the guest house to literally pick up Jacob. By the time all the other men had arrived, Jacob was comfortably seated in the living room.

The men grabbed coffee and bagels, and took some time to talk among themselves. After ten minutes, Adam, Liam, and David moved to the large television that hung on the wall. "If I could have your attention, please," David said, looking around the room. "Today I'm going to lead us in prayer and then turn it over to Liam and Adam."

After David prayed over the group, Adam stepped forward. "Many of you know that our friend Jacob has touched the world for Jesus. He is known to many as The Preacher, and you've all heard his testimony, which is truly inspirational."

"For me, listening to his preaching online made an impact that, along with his encouragement, led me to salvation," Liam continued. "Adam and I have decided to honor Jacob for his humility, love, and compassion. We honor him as an example of what it means to put God above all else."

The screen came on, and *Jacob's Haven* appeared in bold print above an interactive website. It was impressive, obviously designed by an excellent web designer.

"This site contains every known sermon given by Jacob, in video and audio," Adam said. "People will have the opportunity to listen to him preach the Word of God on any media platform they choose, wherever they go. There's also a bulletin board where organizations looking for volunteers or having special events can post. You can click on the map to see every church in your area, along with their service times and a brief description of their beliefs. There are several Q&A pages to help people who are seeking guidance, as well as additional resources."

Liam walked over to Jacob, who stared at the screen with tears of happiness in his eyes. "There is also a tab for donations, one hundred percent of which will fund Jacob's Haven. We've already purchased two abandoned hotels, one in South Phoenix, the other in Casa Grande, and they will be converted into safe living spaces for homeless families. These two hotels total three hundred and twelve rooms, and we've already started coordinating with state and local governments to have vital resources available for these families."

Adam smiled at the men. "Our goal, as it evolves and grows, is to make Jacob's Haven safe places that provide security, tutors, clothing, job support, healthcare, and opportunities to attend church services, transportation, and counseling. A haven is a place of safety and refuge, and that's what these places will provide—everything these families need to get back on their feet." He glanced at Jacob. "Street ministry is a passion of Jacob's, and this will become his legacy for generations, in word and deed."

Everyone clapped, and Liam asked Jacob if he wanted to say anything.

With his blanket he wiped the tears sliding down his face. "What you all have done for me is more than any man can hope for or dream," he whispered. "But then I remember our Father in heaven and realize that with him all things are possible. He surpasses our understanding of what is even imaginable in our life, when we put him first. What we thought we wanted, we don't want anymore. What we thought was success—money, access, and things—we understand is worthless unless it's about him."

He took a sip of the Gatorade in his hand. "I'm blessed to have known each of you. It's been an honor to live my last days in the company of friends who support each other. I can promise you that there will be tough times, challenging moments when you question yourself and God. Times when you will crave the *why* of his purpose so much that you can only focus on it, missing everything else he's showing you. We're all human. But understand at the end of it all, when you're falling, put your eyes back on him. He will guide you through the obstacles, put you on the right path, and deliver you from your circumstances. I can testify to that truth and so can you, as you see me standing here in front of you all."

Jacob sat back in his seat, exhausted but with joy in his eyes.

———

When the meeting ended, the men each shook Jacob's hand and leaned down to hug him.

Jacob didn't speak again until everyone had left except Liam. "Thank you for giving me the opportunity to make a difference when I'm gone," he said. "What gives me the greatest joy is seeing the two of you working together to reach people, showing them what it means to be a Christian. I would ask how you managed to pull all this off in less than a month, but I know that answer. I've seen what you can do firsthand when you're motivated. Now with God for you, who can be against you?" He smiled, happiness radiating from within him.

Adam thought of the road they had each traveled to end up where they stood right now. Some people would call it coincidence, but that was just an easy excuse for those who refused to accept God's purpose as absolute truth.

Adam and Liam carried Jacob back down to the guesthouse, returning him to his place at the table.

Sadie helped him to the bedroom, and when she returned, motioned for them to follow her outside. "I'm not sure how much longer he can hang on," she said quietly. "You may want to stick close to home for the next few days. I've been wrong before, but just to be safe I thought you'd want to know."

They thanked her and walked up to Liam's car.

"You have the rematch event next weekend," Liam said. "When do you have to be at the casino?"

"Contractually, I'm obligated to be there by noon on Thursday for the first press conference. There's a bunch of PR stuff Thursday, then the event starts Friday. It's broken into three sessions, one each day, ending on Sunday. I'll be gone for four days total. Lizzy's flying down on Friday evening after she drops the kids at her parents' house."

Liam sighed. "You had Ramos Copperwood's team look at the contract. Are there no loopholes to change the dates, reschedule, anything?"

"No, not without lying about my health, which I'm not doing. There's a strong possibility when I say goodbye to him on Thursday, it'll be the last time we speak. But there's nothing I can do. Jacob and I talked about it the other day, and he think's my concern is silly. He told me that my being home or away isn't going to change the outcome, which is the truth. It's not like we'll have advanced notice alerting us to stand by him when the end comes."

"No," Liam agreed. "And, my friend, you've been standing by him the whole time."

CHAPTER 22

OMEGA

Adam awoke the next morning to Lizzy sitting on the edge of the bed as she gently nudged his shoulder. She was crying. "Sadie was just here. She went to wake Jacob this morning, but he was gone. Sweetheart, I'm so sorry."

Already? He'd really thought they'd have more time. "He's at peace now. No pain, only God's love." He started to sob, and she lay down next to him with her chest to his back. Stroking his hair, she held him as the spasms of his diaphragm shook them both.

When he stopped crying, Lizzy said, "Why don't you have a shower and get dressed. I'll talk with Sadie about what happens next, then call Beth." She kissed his forehead, then squeezed his hand and left.

Adam rolled onto his back and stared at the ceiling, unable to think. He grabbed his phone off the nightstand, disconnecting it from the charging cord. Its bright light made him squint as he typed out a text. He analyzed what he'd written, wanting the announcement to be as dignified as the man. *Our friend Jacob has passed away, leaving the pain behind, to find the only true peace that is our Father in heaven. I will update everyone when arrangements have been made to celebrate his life. God bless.* He sent it to everyone in the men's group and Caliste, then posted it to the Jacob's Haven website, from which it would be automatically posted to the social media platforms.

He set the phone back on the nightstand and returned his gaze to the ceiling. In no hurry to start the day, knowing that once downstairs the reality would be undeniable, Adam lay there for a while listening to the buzz of his phone vibrating as each new text arrived.

Then he remembered that Lizzy was downstairs alone. He got out of bed, showered and shaved, and then sat in the chair by the window. Bowing his head, he prayed for guidance, and thanked God for his mercy and grace and for sending Jacob to help him find his way back. He grabbed his phone from the nightstand, dropped it into his pocket, and headed for the kitchen.

Lizzy and Beth sat at the island sipping coffee, while Liam stood at the windows, looking toward the guest house. The kids had to be somewhere, but he couldn't hear them. Sadness seemed to saturate the air.

Liam caught Adam's eye and pointed to the coffee machine.

Adam nodded. Normally, he would take his coffee to the guest house to sit outside with Jacob. They'd talked about everything under the sun—theology, history, sports, travel, and life. He always looked forward to that, knowing he walked away with more knowledge each time. A good teacher made a person excited about learning. Today he and Liam stood by the back windows with their coffee.

Liam squeezed his shoulder as they looked out over the pool. "I didn't think it would happen so fast. I would have stuck around longer yesterday. How you holding up?"

Adam looked down at his cup. "I'm numb. I thought we would have more time too, but really, no amount of time would have been enough—at least for me. He was ready to go home. I hope when my time comes, I have his courage."

"Do you know what he wanted for a funeral—sorry, celebration of life?"

Adam sighed. "He never said. He talked far more about living than dying, and rarely did he want to discuss himself. It was always about everyone else."

Adam topped off his and Liam's coffee and the two walked down to check on Sadie.

She gave them a half smile. "I went to get him up for his morning coffee and fresh air, but he had already passed during the night. He looked so peaceful that I thought he was just asleep." She teared up and went into the guest house, and Liam and Adam followed. She grabbed her coffee from the counter, then took a seat at the table, leaving Jacob's cup in front of his favorite seat. "Have you decided on a funeral home?" she asked Adam.

"No. Do you have any suggestions?"

"Twin Palms is nice and not far. I can give them a call if you'd like and have them send someone over."

Adam stared down the hall toward where his friend's body lay. "Yeah, please. I'd really appreciate it. Then Liam and I can follow them back to the funeral home and figure out where we go from here." He swallowed some coffee. "Jacob wouldn't talk much about dying. I tried asking him a few times what he wanted after he passed, but he always found a way to change the subject. Did he share with you how he wanted his life celebrated?"

She got up and took three envelopes from a cabinet—one addressed to Liam, another to Adam, and the third titled *Upon My Death*. "Last week we had a talk. I convinced him how important it was to write down his wishes. I reminded him that it wasn't fair to you if he didn't."

Adam opened the third envelope. It contained a one-page letter and a bundle of cash. He set the cash on the table, then began reading the letter out loud.

To my brothers in Christ, Adam and Liam,

Thank you for everything you have done for me in my last days. Know that I died having people around me who I loved and cherished. Please tell Beth and Lizzy that their willingness to allow me into your lives was a true blessing, one of the greatest gifts I've ever received. I could not have asked for a kinder, more compassionate person to look after me in my final days than Sadie. Thank you for the gift of passing away not alone but spending my final moments with you all. The money is what's left of the ten thousand you gave me in Miss Mabel's kitchen. I thank God I chose to stay. God certainly showed us the way. Upon my death, please have a simple ceremony. Those who would like to speak, allow them the opportunity. If you can, bury me in a simple coffin in a place by a tree or water, both if possible. The only other request is that you play some of Miles' music during the ceremony. Hearing him play when we were in New Orleans moved me. I'll leave the rest up to you, whatever is easiest. Please don't go to a lot of trouble. I love you all.

Love, Jacob

Adam looked down at the stack of hundred-dollar bills. Most of the ten thousand remained, and he smiled, thinking of what Jacob would want. He slid the stack of bills toward Sadie. "I want you to have this as a small token of how much we appreciated you taking such good care of our friend. It's what he would want, so it's not up for discussion."

Sadie's mouth opened as she looked down at the stack of cash. Then she smiled at Adam. "Thank you. He was a special man. Never in all my thirty years of nursing experience have I cared for anyone like him. But I want you to donate this money to Jacob's Haven. He told me what you all are doing, and I want to be a part of it. I've seen the other side working in hospitals over the years. He shared with me everything you all have planned, and I can't wait to see it. That's God's work, and I want to be a part of it."

Adam grinned back and nodded.

Sadie made the call, and they sat drinking coffee and waiting for the people to arrive from the funeral home. Soon a large black van stopped at the end of the driveway, and Liam went up to the house to let Beth and Lizzy know they were headed over to the funeral home. Adam walked back to the bedroom with Sadie and the two men who would transport the body.

The blanket was pulled up to Jacob's neck, with his lifeless body barely noticeable underneath the thick duvet. Adam stood at the edge of the bed, staring down at him. It dawned on him that the flesh that betrays humans is all that's left behind. The spirit is gone, reunited with its creator. He found comfort in Jacob's words filling his mind. Those weren't words Adam would have strung together months ago. Even in death Jacob continued to impact his thoughts.

Liam and Jacob followed the van, Liam driving and Adam checking his phone. Twenty-seven texts and three calls. He scrolled through the texts, most from guys in their men's group asking what they could do to help. All asked to be notified when the arrangements were made for Jacob's celebration of life. David asked that Adam call when he had time or if he needed to talk. Two of his voicemail messages were business related and the third was from Caliste. Adam listened to Caliste's message, then laughed.

"What's so funny?" Liam asked.

"You have to hear this. It's Caliste." He put the phone on speaker and played the message: "It's me. We're leaving here shortly. You know Miss Mabel won't fly. She doesn't trust *steel birds*—her words, not mine. She's at the store with Clayton now, picking up a few things. Then we'll be on the road, should be there by Monday evening. Miss Mabel has never stepped a foot outside Louisiana, so please pray for us. Text me the best hotel close to your house when you have a chance. No hurry, we'll be in the car for two days. Sorry for your loss. Jacob was a true man of God. I wish we could have had more time with him."

This time both laughed.

When they reached the funeral home, the owner, a Mr. Cunningham, showed them their casket options. It was a strange place to be, a large showroom with different models of coffins and the prices attached to each on an information sheet.

Adam followed Jacob's instructions, choosing a simple coffin. Next, they were shown a map of the available burial sites. Adam described Jacob's request—by water or a tree, and Mr. Cunningham pointed out a lot. It was the most expensive one, but it was under a large tree by a lake. It was perfect.

When Adam and Liam got back to the house, everyone was gone. Adam checked his phone and found a text from Lizzy: *We took Lilly to her game. Beth and all the kids are with me. We'll be back in a few hours. Text me if you need anything. Sadie left. She asked that you reach out to her when you know the plan for Jacob's celebration of life. I love you.*

At first, he was surprised that Lizzy would still take Lilly to the game. But then it seemed like the best thing she could have done. There was no reason for Lilly to miss her game, and the next few days would be filled with people coming and going from the house. He decided to keep Miss Mabel's visit a surprise for the kids, and that reminded him to text Caliste for a favor concerning the funeral.

Liam sat down on the couch and turned on the television. "Adam, you've got to see this," he said after a few moments.

When Adam turned around, Liam was off the couch and in front of the television pointing at the rolling tally of donations in the bottom left-hand corner. The rectangle read $318,907 and was still spinning. Every time a donation came in, the rectangle's border would flash red. When they scrolled through all the social media feeds, thousands of comments had come in. People wanted to contribute to the cause. The two sat back on the couch, reading the messages as they popped up in real time. Simultaneously they watched as the number in the corner continued to climb.

Adam spoke with David, and it was decided that the service would be held at the church. They had the perfect venue. It was free to anyone who had a need, and after the service, everyone could gather under the pavilions to enjoy a nice lunch. Lizzy hired the mother of one of Beth's students—a woman who owned a catering business and was a member of the church—for the event. The rest of the weekend was spent visiting with people who stopped by to pay their respects. The television never went off, displaying the messages coming in from all over the world and the donations, which neared a million dollars when Adam turned out the lights on Sunday night.

Lizzy, Beth, and the kids were back at school on Monday, leaving Adam and Liam to work. They took a break in the afternoon to visit Paul for a late lunch. He had another week left in rehab but could leave with family for a few hours at a time, so they took him to the local pizza parlor.

Paul hadn't spent much time with Jacob, but he seemed saddened. "I'd like to pay my respects if I could and be at the funeral, if that's okay with you."

Adam nodded, glad that he wanted to be part of the celebration. "I'll talk to the desk nurse when we get back, work out the arrangements."

———

That night, Miss Mabel, Clayton, and Caliste arrived. The back of Clayton's Suburban contained, among other things, three huge coolers packed full. Miss Mabel had brought enough food to feed twenty people for at least a few days. The kids were thrilled, and spent all their time at the kitchen table on Tuesday, watching Miss Mabel cook. And when she wasn't cooking, she'd tell stories while playing board games with them. Adam was glad they'd agreed to stay at the house instead of in a hotel.

It was a wonderful time shared under sad circumstances, but the family was together, and it was a time to celebrate life. That was what Jacob would have wanted. Everything had come together seamlessly. David handled all the logistics at the church, which was a huge help. One of the senior pastors agreed to officiate the service, and Adam would deliver the eulogy. In accordance with Jacob's wishes, anyone who wanted to speak would have the opportunity.

The smell of Miss Mabel's food pulled him from his thoughts on Tuesday evening. Everyone was gathering in the kitchen to eat. Adam had lost track of time while sitting by the pool in the chair he used to spend so much time in, drinking coffee with his friend. Earlier in the day, they set the patio tables end to end, making one long table on the porch so everyone could sit together.

He watched as the kids brought out the dishes and set them on the table. Lizzy was waving for him to come, and he stood and looked down at the chair where Jacob once sat. "I miss you, my friend," he said before heading for the porch.

At the table, Adam asked Miss Mabel to say grace, and when she was finished, the food was passed around. At one end of the table sat a plate that went untouched, a glass beside it. It was an empty seat that no one else could ever fill.

CHAPTER 23

FAMILY

Lizzy was still asleep when Adam got up the next morning. Careful not to disturb her, he closed the bedroom door quietly easing it into the frame. It was just after five, and he had laid awake next to her for as long as he could before giving up on sleep. The smell of chicory-infused coffee caught his nose when he reached the top of the stairs, and he smiled. He couldn't remember a time when Miss Mabel didn't beat him to the coffee.

She was sitting at the kitchen table staring across the living room at the website on the television. "Child, coffee's ready," she said without taking her eyes off the screen. "That creamer you like I set out on the counter."

Adam poured his coffee, taking in the smell as it steamed up from the cup, then sat down in a chair that he could see the TV from. "What time do you get up in the morning?"

Miss Mabel looked at him. "Whenever the good Lord opens my eyes. How you holdin' up?"

Adam stared into his coffee. "In the short time I got to spend with him, he taught me so much. I don't know how to communicate just how much. I can't find the words for the eulogy. It's impossible to sum up Jacob in a few pieces of paper."

Miss Mabel pointed to the TV. "You already did. You're showing the world who he was as a man of God. People who never knew him going to hear his story in the preaching. Then you done went and made it about the heart he had for the homeless, people suffering hard times. When you get up on that stage, child, you just let the Lord take you where he wants to go. Don't write nothing down. The words, they fittin' to come from the good Lord. You watch and see."

There was wisdom in her suggestion—as usual. Really, that was probably the best thing to do since he hadn't managed to write anything good enough. Every time he tried, the words didn't sound right. What he settled on barely qualified as decent.

"You know, when it was just Jacob and me in the kitchen—you were sleeping—I told him to check his heart, make sure God didn't want him back on that stage preaching. Sometimes God just shows you how big he is, and sure enough he showed us. When you all were leaving, I held Jacob behind a few ticks, told him that God sent him to pull you from the darkness and into the light. I was right about him helping you find the light, praise Jesus. My prayers all these years came true. I can see it in you." She rested her hand on his, her eyes full of joy.

Adam stood and kissed her on the forehead. "It means so much, you being here for the kids, Lizzy, and me. You can always stay a few months at a time. This is your home as well."

Miss Mabel smiled brightly. "My home is in New Orleans. You saved my home when you bought Jack's house. I never thanked you, knew it was too much a sore subject back then. Never was there a good time to bring it up. Seemed I'd be tearing a scab open on a wound fittin' to heal. I know why you bought it, though, especially after what happened, what we seen. You stepped in for Clayton, Caliste, and me—saved our home, the history we knew. Some of them memories we wanted to forget, some we never wanted to let go."

She nodded. "You gave us that. The house that holds our history in the place we call home. I know you bought it when you didn't have nothing, from the dead man who took every dime you had. But you made it happen, praise God. Thank you, child, for loving us that much. Now, go on and get ready. I need to put the stove on."

Adam refilled his coffee and left Miss Mabel to work in the kitchen. Soon the smell of her cooking would have everybody in the house up. He walked to the television to check the website. Without his contacts in, he needed to get closer to see the number in the corner.

$3,190,739? He couldn't believe it. He'd expected the contributions to slow down, but they had sped up and more than doubled from the night before. When he started reading the messages, many about the celebration of life, he realized there was going to be a lot more people than they planned for.

He went back upstairs and texted David, telling him to look at the Jacob's Haven website. There was no way of knowing how many people would show up to celebrate Jacob's life. Then he texted Liam to see if there was a way to look at the website's analytics to determine how many people commented that they were attending the service. It was Liam's job to coordinate with the web team, and Adam didn't understand the language they spoke.

David called back since he wasn't much of a texter, and they decided to move the food into one of the buildings, limiting access to invitation only. He also suggested that they hire a few off-duty officers he knew to handle the traffic and security just in case.

Adam woke Lizzy to fill her in on what was happening.

She smiled when he finished. "Honey, let it go. We plan the best we can, and whatever happens, we deal with it. Don't stress yourself. There's nothing you can do. It's out of our control."

By the time they dressed and went downstairs, the kids, Caliste, and Clayton were already at the kitchen table eating. They were handed plates piled high with creamy grits, eggs, biscuits, and thick bacon. Not wanting to interrupt, they listened to the conversation between Theo, Lilly, Caliste, and Clayton. Caliste was telling stories about what it was like to be raised by Miss Mabel and some of the trouble he got into, mostly with the help of Clayton.

They were just about finished breakfast when Liam, Beth, and the kids showed up with their special guest. They'd picked up Miles at the airport. Caliste introduced him to everyone, and Miss Mabel handed each of the new arrivals a fixed plate. Everyone knew to take the plate, except Beth who was trying to get Miss Mabel's attention as she walked away.

Liam stepped between the two, rotating Beth away and whispering, "You don't want any part of that, honey. Just eat it."

Adam thanked Miles for coming, explained how much Jacob loved his music, and filled him in on the structure of the celebration. He was to play whatever came to his heart.

———

When they reached the church, David met everyone in the office parking lot, then walked them into the sanctuary using the stage entrance to avoid the crowd. Seats had been cordoned off in the front row for the family. The sanctuary, built to hold thirty-five hundred people, was already full to capacity, and people stood in the back.

Adam stood backstage with Miles and Senior Pastor Ashton Morrison while David handled all the logistics. Miles mic'd up, then walked out onto the stage and began playing "Amazing Grace." Within ten seconds, all the talking among audience members ceased.

Miles played two more songs, "At the Cross" and "Go Tell it on the Mountain," then introduced Pastor Morrison before taking his seat next to Caliste. The pastor invited everyone to pray, then read three Scripture passages that talked about the significance of God's love. He spoke for a few minutes about Jacob, what it meant to be a vessel for God's Word, and the ups and downs that a life of ministry can bring but how faith in his Word was the answer in the best and worst of times.

When he was finished, Miles played again as photos of Jacob from over the years flashed on the screen behind him. It was a moving experience that included stills of him on stage preaching, sometimes in front of thousands, other times in a room with thirty people. When the presentation finished, the pastor prayed again and then invited Adam to the stage.

Adam walked up to the podium and stood looking out at the crowd, amazed at the number of people who came to celebrate Jacob's life. Sure, some were newly introduced, but many had been touched years ago by the power of his preaching. Taking a breath, he took Miss Mabel's advice and surrendered his tongue to the Lord.

The words just came, and sometimes he didn't know what he was saying until the words came out of his mouth. Adam spoke about how Jacob had lost all his worldly possessions, was forced to live homeless, jailed, betrayed, sick, dying, and filled with pain, yet never did he lose faith in his Father. And that, despite his circumstances, he received far more than he ever lost, a far greater measure than man could quantify. Then he described how Jacob impacted all those around him with humility and love. When Adam finished, everyone stood clapping—not for him, he was sure, but for Jacob.

David invited anyone who wanted to say a few words to speak, and for two hours, people shared stories of how Jacob had impacted their life. Liam then went to the podium and announced that they would need to end due to time restrictions but that anyone who still wanted to share could do so on the website. As the service ended, the family members and the families of the guys from men's group moved to the building adjacent to the sanctuary for lunch. From there, they headed to the cemetery for an informal service.

David prayed, Liam shared a few Scripture verses, and the kids all placed bouquets of flowers around the sign where the tombstone would eventually be placed. Everyone watched as the coffin was lowered, then each person threw a handful of dirt into the grave. After a few moments of silence, everyone headed back to their cars, leaving the body of their friend under a tree by a lake, fulfilling his final wish.

"Dad, why did Jacob want to be by a tree and next to water?" Theo asked on the ride home.

Adam thought for a few moments before answering. "I don't know, buddy, but I'm sure he had a reason. Maybe something having to do with Scripture."

The remainder of the day was spent talking and eating. It was a time for family—family defined as the ones who could be counted on whatever the circumstances, bound not by blood but acceptance, forgiveness, and love for each other. During dinner, Miss Mabel surprised everyone with the news that she and Clayton would stay with the kids, while Caliste, Beth, Lizzy, and Liam all went to Las Vegas with Adam.

After dinner, Lizzy and Beth prepared lesson plans for their substitutes, and Caliste, Liam, and Adam retreated to Adam's office to discuss their plans for Jacob's Haven. The next hotel they purchased would be in New Orleans, and Caliste, who was happy to have the opportunity to make a difference, would play a large part in the process. So many people in the Crescent City needed the services Jacob's Haven would provide. The donations kept coming in on the website, with the attention Adam was getting on social media since the interview helping to spread Jacob's story. Liam reminded everyone that they had to be careful to not outgrow their capital, to be methodical and careful and not to overextend themselves.

"This event will put you in front of the media all weekend," Caliste said. "Three days are being broadcast on pay-per-view and over the net, plus Thursday's media day. You have a perfect platform, and we need to take advantage of it beyond the interviews and make sure Jacob's Haven continues to trend on social media. We don't want to leave it up to only journalists putting their spin on the story to generate more views. How can we use the opportunity to send a clear, concise message to the viewers?"

"We already have a ton of celebrities, athletes, and some church leaders and politicians reposting and endorsing the cause. Some are even doing match campaigns, donating up to a certain amount of whatever is raised in a specified period of time," Liam said. "That's one of the reasons social media is on fire and the donation total is up to over $6 million. Maybe we can figure out a way to trigger more involvement from them so we can reach their followers. Until now the plan has been for Adam to discuss, as often as he can, our goal for Jacob's Haven, naming the website whenever possible. The casino refused to add the logo or web address to any of their media, so that's not an option. Chad will be there filming a follow-up to the interview, so that should be huge for us. I asked him to wait a week before airing it, to reignite attention for the cause, which he was happy to do."

Caliste smiled. "Okay, then we can go old school. They can't tell you what to wear. Let's have your sweatshirt make a statement. That's your billboard for the entire event from the first day to the last. We can change it up each day, and can also hand out free T-shirts. That way people are walking around Vegas advertising for us. When they go home, they'll be taking the shirts with them and spreading the cause. The T-shirts may not have a huge impact, but they'll be enough to get attention. What do you think?"

Adam looked at his watch. "Do we have enough time to have shirts printed by tomorrow night or Friday morning?"

"Leave that to me," Liam said. "I know a guy who can handle the volume for us. He's in LA, so he can hand deliver them to us. We just need to figure out what we want on them."

Adam considered that. "Well, we need to keep it simple and direct, say what it is we're trying to accomplish. How about we put Jacob's Haven and our logo on the front of the shirt, and on the back the outline of a house with *Shelter, Food, Education, Safety,* and *Healthcare* listed. Then in bold under the house, *Help Build a Home.* Let's make the shirts red with white letters and a white cross on the sleeve with *God Is Love* under it."

"That sounds perfect," Liam said. "Direct and to the point, no room for confusion."

"I agree it sends the right message," Caliste added, "but for your hoodie, are you sure the casino won't make you cover any advertising?"

"That won't be a problem. One of the conditions of the contract Ramos made is that I can wear whatever I choose. Originally it was so I wouldn't have to wear their logo or endorse another company, but now it'll allow me to advertise the charity."

"It sounds like we have a plan," Liam said, "but let's be ready to adapt based on circumstances and opportunity while we're there. I think we're good for tonight, so I'm heading home. I'll call my guy Jason in LA and make this order happen. I'm thinking five thousand shirts. You want the same thing on the hoodies?"

Adam thought for a few moments. "I think five thousand will work. We can hire a few people to hand them out on the strip as well. I'll text you what to put on my hoodie. I need to think for a few minutes. I can't have anything on the back since I'm sitting the whole time."

Caliste and Liam said their goodbyes and left Adam alone for the first time in a while. Within a few minutes he'd determined what he wanted on his sweatshirt and texted it to Liam. He then texted Lizzy that he'd come inside in a few minutes.

He pulled Jacob's Bible from the top drawer of his desk, prayed and gave thanks to God, then opened to the Gospel of John and began to read.

In the beginning was the Word, and the Word was with God, and the Word was God. He was with God in the beginning. Through him all things are made; without him nothing was made that has been made. In him was life, and that life was the light of all mankind. The light shines in the darkness, and the darkness has not overcome it.

Chapter 24

The Event

They arrived at the hotel just before ten a.m. the next morning and were greeted by the casino executives, who welcomed them personally before introducing their assigned hosts. There were three hosts, one for each couple and for Caliste, who would be their point of contact for anything they needed.

After the pleasantries were finished, a recap of the day's itinerary was discussed in the VIP lounge. The hosts then escorted them to their suites, where their bags were waiting along with huge welcome baskets. Adam had an hour to rest and dress before the mandatory media time that started at noon. Lizzy left Adam, joining Beth, Liam, and Caliste who were meeting Jason in the lobby to pick up the shirts.

Lizzy returned to the suite with the sweatshirts Adam would wear over the course of the four-day event. She was already wearing one of the T-shirts, which had turned out even nicer than Adam expected. "Liam ordered messenger bags with the website printed on them," she said as she sat down on the couch with him. "He's using one of the small conference rooms as a distribution center, and hired some people who are now rolling the shirts and packing them in the bags. Liam, Caliste, Beth, and I all have credentials so we can hand them out at the media events. The rest are being handed out all along the strip. Liam also put the shirt on the site. Anyone donating fifty dollars or more gets one for free. Seems like a pretty good idea. People love free stuff, even if it's not technically free."

As noon neared, Adam showered and put on his usual jeans, Air Force Ones, and hoodie.

"How do you think the casino will react to your advertising Jesus and Jacob's Haven?" Lizzy asked as she looked him over.

"They may try to make an issue of it, but there's not much more they can do than make empty threats. The casino stands to make millions. They know my contract, and I doubt they're stupid enough to push hard." He stared out through the windows at the skyline and the mountains in the distance. "Baby, the truth is I'm not looking forward to playing," he admitted. "If it wasn't for us getting our message out on a big stage, I probably would have backed out of the event. This is going to be my last match, the last event of my career."

Casino management didn't even acknowledge Adam's sweatshirt. Adam spent the afternoon answering questions about his faith, poker, Chad's interview, Jacob, Jacob's Haven, and what caused the open declaration of his Christianity. He answered most questions, politely refusing only the more personal ones about his family. Afterward, they had dinner at Jamie's, the newest fine dining experience at the hotel, where he did the required photos with the chef and manager. Those would be used in advertising for the next few months, until someone else took his place.

After dinner was the face-off, which was set up like the press conference before a big fight. Adam and Alan answered questions on stage, sitting at a long table separated by the head of casino promotions and his staff. The media could ask whatever questions they wished, and Adam was not looking forward to it. Alan relished these types of situations, and there was no telling what he would say or how he would behave. Adam had to stay calm, cool, and collected no matter what. He couldn't allow Alan to get under his skin. In the past, that had never been an issue, but that was before the scheme to go after his family.

Adam went to one of the green rooms to wait for the main event. The announcer called him out, and read off his accomplishments as he crossed the stage and sat down at the table. The crowd was a mix of journalists, social media influencers, and fans, and he was surprised by how much applause and noise he received. Apparently, he had a lot more fans backing him than he'd anticipated. Sprinkled among the crowd were some of the red shirts that were handed out earlier in the day. The orator for the evening asked Adam a few general questions about his excitement level. Adam thanked everyone who was making the event possible—the hotel, casino, and all the fans of poker.

Then Alan was called out. His intro included a hard-hitting baseline threaded with a rap dedicated to him winning the event. Lyrics filled with offensive language and multiple rhymes illustrating how Alan would kill Adam in the rematch, boomed over the speakers. When Alan appeared, four blonde twenty-somethings were all around him. He wore a shirt bearing the picture of Adam with the college girls at The Blue Note, along with his customary jeans, gators, sunglasses, and copious jewelry. He looked more like a late-1990s rapper than a poker player.

Alan kissed each of the ladies, then walked onto the stage, faced the crowd, and pointed at his shirt. Adam's hands fisted, but he reminded himself that he needed to pray for Alan. Adam had made this event about Jacob, and he had made a statement to the world about his commitment to Jesus, so the spotlight was on him. A lot of people would be looking for an opportunity to destroy what he was trying to build for the kingdom of God.

Adam stood and walked to the middle of the table to shake Alan's hand. Alan turned his back, refusing Adam's outstretched hand, and went to his seat. There he sat down, pulled out his phone, and took pictures of the crowd, then started posting them on social media. Many of the audience members pulled out their phones.

Adam determined that he needed to ignore Alan and let him be a clown. It was a grueling two hours of video bits showing them competing against each other over the years. Then the announcer would ask what each player was thinking during that sequence of hands or when they held up the winning cards with stacks of hundred-dollar bills surrounding them.

Adam answered the questions as best he could, congratulating Alan when he made good calls. Every time he spoke, Alan pulled out his phone and posted something nasty about Adam. He could hear reactions of laughter or shock in the audience, but was unable to see what was posted. Finally, as they were nearing the end, the orator asked Alan what concerns he had going against Adam tomorrow.

He looked up from his phone at Adam, then made a point to stare at Lizzy in the front row. "I'm not worried about Adam. He's a has-been. His luck's run out. Everyone knows I'm the better player. I'm worried about his wife. That poor little hottie has to deal with him running around behind her back with all these women half her age." He pointed at his shirt. "I guess he's one of those men who resorts to college girls half his age to make himself feel wanted or important. We all know if he didn't have money, they wouldn't give him a second look. His poor wife, Lizzy, though. If she wants the attention of a real man who appreciates things aged well, she can give me a call."

Lizzy was now trying to get to the stage, but Liam and Beth had her arm in arm, half walking and half carrying her out of the auditorium. Caliste walked to the edge of the stage and hung out by the stairs just in case.

Adam put his hands on the table and pushed himself up, then after a moment sat back down in his chair. "Alan's remarks are unprofessional and require no response. Anyone who cares about the facts can watch the interview that Chad Sterling conducted a month ago. He's an award-winning journalist who many in the poker world know and respect for his commitment to integrity. Everyone here now knows about Jacob's Haven and the man who inspired it. So that there is no misunderstanding, I want to make an announcement. I will match every donation to Jacob's Haven that is submitted between now and the close of the final round Sunday. The limit of the matching donations is the total amount I earn from my heads-up play against Alan."

He glanced at his opponent. "I want to thank Alan for the large donation he is about to make to Jacob's Haven, and I want to thank God for the opportunity to make a real difference in people's lives through the work of Jacob's Haven. I'll see you all tomorrow on the felt. God bless." He stood and walked off the stage as the audience stared in silence.

Outside the room, Adam approached Caliste. "Where's Lizzy? Is she okay?"

"Liam texted me. They're up in your suite. Lizzy's fine." Caliste shook his head. "Man, I have to give you credit. That was tough, but you stayed strong. Alan's lucky Lizzy didn't get a hold of him. She would have beat him down if she made the stage."

Adam chuckled. "There's only two things I'm scared of in this world—God and my wife."

When they reached the suite, Liam was on the phone and Lizzy and Beth were at the table. "I'm so sorry, baby," Adam said. "I didn't see that coming."

Lizzy smiled. "I'm fine. He was trying to get you to make a scene by insulting me. It didn't work."

Liam hung up. "I just got a call from Chad. Did you just offer to match all the donations over the next four days?"

When Adam looked at Lizzy, she was waiting for an explanation. "Yes. I capped it at my total winnings for the rematch."

Lizzy stood up. "Well, okay. Let's hope they max us out. But the next time you make this kind of a decision, we need to have a conversation first. We're a team, you and me. It's not about the money, it's about us being in agreement."

He hadn't considered that. "Absolutely, honey."

———————

Alan sat across the table from Adam, fully focused on the hand. His typical annoying comments were put aside temporarily as he battled Adam's silence. The T-shirt he wore yesterday before had been replaced by a different one to match his Brioni suit.

He was holding a pair of nines, and the flop delivered his third nine of spades, but along with it came a ten of spades and a jack of hearts. Adam had raised pre-flop and Alan called, but now there was a possible straight and flush draw on the table. Alan couldn't let trips go without seeing the turn, watching closely as the dealer flipped the turn, a two of diamonds. That couldn't have helped anyone. Alan was the first to act, but without the table being paired giving him a full house, he had to be careful. Adam bet the pot—$2.6 million—which would put Alan all in if he called.

Alan analyzed the hand, not wanting to lose the first of the three matches and be down to Adam from the start. Each day the players started with $10 million, and the first four hours were pot limit and then switched to no limit. The casino needed to stretch the event out to last as long as possible so they could maximize their return on investment. Whoever won the event got a $5 million kicker as a bonus.

He had trips. There was no way Adam was betting pre-flop at this point with king-queen unless maybe they were suited, or he was riding a bluff. There was always one hand in a heads-up match that was the game changer. Sometimes it was the stack that was affected, other times the confidence. Alan new this was the hand, and he called, believing Adam didn't have a straight and hoping the river wouldn't deliver him a flush. Better yet, if the board paired or a nine came on the river, he couldn't imagine Adam had a better hand.

The board paired with the two of spades, and Alan pumped his fist, returning to his arrogant, narcissistic behavior, yelling and getting his fans fired up. It didn't matter if Adam had a flush or a straight. His full house beat both hands. He flipped his nines over, showing his full house, then stood up facing the crowd to soak in their fever.

Then suddenly his fans stopped cheering. No one was joining him in celebration. He turned and looked down at the table. Lying face up was a pair of jacks. Adam had him beat on the flop with trip jacks. It had never occurred to him that Adam was waiting for a full house with the nut trips on the flop.

Adam walked to the announcers for the recap, taking the time to answer a few questions before leaving. He never looked back at Alan, just walked out with Lizzy, Liam, Beth, and Caliste, who were all wearing the red-and-white T-shirts.

———

Day two brought much longer play, with the match beginning at noon and stretching to nearly eleven p.m. It was an odd day that Adam spent mostly card dead trying to make something happen. Luck and momentum ended with his kings against Alan's aces. Adam had caught a king on the flop, but Alan managed to catch an ace high flush on the river. In poker there was an aspect of luck, the idea being that it's offset by repetition, patience, discipline, and skill. It was far easier to play out to the statistics over time, but heads-up made that more difficult.

Adam had to acknowledge in the post-match interviews that Alan had played well, especially compared to the previous day. It would all come down to the final day of play. Now they sat even, Alan having won $10 million and Adam the same, which meant Sunday put $30 million in play for each player. Someone was going home with $35 million—the $5 million kicker and the other guy's $30 million. Sixty million dollars would be on the felt Sunday morning—$30 million from each player—and this was the scenario the fans wanted. Friday and Saturday were basically a wash. It all came down to the finale.

Instead of dinner out, Adam's team sequestered themselves in his suite, choosing to have one of the chefs prepare their meal. It was a working dinner, with Liam giving updates on the numbers for donations, the website analytics, social media trends, and offers of partnership they were receiving from the corporate community, politicians, and church leaders. It was good for Adam. He sat listening, amazed at the figures. They were up to $24 million on donations and climbing. Anything to keep his mind off the finale and what it would mean to win.

It wasn't about the money or his pride, ego, and competitive spirit. It was all about what that money would do to support Jacob's Haven—the help people would receive. Not to mention the number of people who would be introduced to Jesus.

"Let's hold any decisions about partnerships or endorsements until after tomorrow," Adam said. "You need to use your skills to vet them, dig deep, before we agree to allow anyone to be a part of what we're doing. I don't care how much they have or what they promise. It's our responsibility to protect the organization and our commitment. We can't let anything negatively impact our vision."

"I wouldn't have it any other way," Liam agreed. "No stone will go unturned when and if we decide to accept any funds or help from the corporate community or politicians. There's an architect firm that contacted us. They volunteered to provide some building plans free of charge, in case we need to build a facility in an area that doesn't have a suitable hotel to purchase. I told them to put together some concepts for us. Other than that, I've scheduled meetings for everything else starting a week from Monday. I thought everyone could use the rest. I know Paul comes home Monday and you'll want to spend some time with him."

"It'll be good for Paul when he gets back, being a part of something like Jacob's Haven," Beth said. "The positivity will keep him uplifted."

Adam nodded. "He also understands the social media potential. He used to drive me crazy with ideas on how to utilize social media to enhance my revenue. Now he'll have his opportunity, only for a very different reason. I plan to ease him into it and make sure he's around us as much as possible. He'll be staying in the guest house until the time is right for him to go back to living alone. I had the bed donated, Lizzy modernized it a bit for someone his age, and I think it will be good for him to be around the family for a while."

Lizzy set her drink down and looked from Liam to Adam. "You know, I would have never believed we would be sitting here, supporting your vision—with you working together for God's purpose instead of your own, as Jacob would say. You both have abilities that will be incredibly useful in building this charity and helping people. It's awesome to see what God had in his plan for your talents and gifts."

Liam chuckled. "Well, I can only speak for myself when I say I'm a work in progress with a direction forward, but I understand what you mean. I can't wait to see where we end up."

Caliste stood, raising his glass. "A toast to the future. May God bless us, guide us, pick us up when we fall, and remind us to walk with him in everything we do."

———

It was after midnight when everyone left, leaving Lizzy and Adam alone for the first time since the day started. As they lay in bed holding each other, she said, "I want you to know that whether you win or lose in the finale tomorrow, it won't change the man you've become. I'm so proud of you and so are the kids. If Jacob was here, he'd tell you the same thing. Earlier today, Beth was sharing with me that for the first time in their marriage, Liam is talking to her about his work.

He's sharing his ideas about Jacob's Haven with her, and she says their marriage is starting to feel like a real partnership."

Adam kissed her cheek. "If you would have told me that Liam and I would be baptized on the same day by The Preacher, I would have called you a liar. I'm starting to realize what Jacob meant when he said that once you accept you're not in control, everything becomes clearer. You recognize the amazing things God does in your life, big and small." With a smile, he went on, "I enjoy my eyes being open to the truth more and more every day. I think Liam feels it as well. It offers him the same peace and excitement that it does me, seeing not what I'll do next but what God will do next."

They lay there a while longer until Lizzy fell asleep, then Adam gently lifted her arm and rolled to his side. He wasn't sure when sleep came for him, but he remembered his last thought. It wasn't about the finale or what the day would bring. He was thinking of Theo's question about where Jacob wanted to be buried. Why by a tree and water? Maybe time would reveal the answer, or maybe he would never know.

CHAPTER 25

WALK IT OUT

Adam sat at the table eating eggs benedict, fruit, turkey sausage, and toast, waiting for Lizzy to join him. They had slept longer than planned—it was almost nine—and they were meeting everyone at nine thirty in the media room for final interviews.

Lizzy came to the table and uncovered her Denver omelet, toast, and fruit. "Honey, you always tell me you never get nervous," she said, "but are you nervous about this finale?"

Adam considered that. "No. There are times when you win and times when you lose, that's part of the game. Losing is a statistical reality that you accept sometimes no matter how good you play. Someone can get lucky at an opportune time, your cards can run cold, or there can be a bad beat. But I'm going into this today knowing that whatever happens is God's will. All I can do is walk it out."

After breakfast, they walked to the green room designated for Adam. Lizzy, Beth, Liam, and Caliste watched as he sat answering questions from the different journalists rotating into the room. There were questions about Jacob's Haven, Alan, Adam's plans for the future, whether he was really leaving the poker world, and his strategy for the finale. He answered them all except for the ones that included Alan's attack on his character and family. His answer to those questions was always the same—that he had already addressed those issues and had no further comment.

Chad Sterling was the last person to interview him, and he was allotted the most time. He asked poker questions, and touched on the finale and what it would mean to beat Alan. But really, he focused on the human-interest part of the story, wanting to know how Jacob's Haven came to be, about Jacob as a friend, and about Adam's Christian beliefs.

After they finished, the sound of Alan being announced radiated through the auditorium. Caliste called everyone to prayer, and Chad stuck around to join them. He identified himself as a non-practicing Christian and mentioned that he planned to attend church next Sunday for the first time in twenty years. Everyone encouraged him, then went to find their seats, leaving Adam to wait for the final words bringing him to the table.

Adam stood alone, thinking about his future. This would be the last time he'd play the game professionally. He had found his calling, and it was time to focus his energy on that and his family.

He was called out, and cheers erupted as he made his way to the table. Again he thanked God for the blessings in his life. There were far more red shirts in the crowd this day, and that brought a smile to his face. Before sitting, he faced the audience and pointed to the front of his sweatshirt, which read *God Is Love, John 3:16. JacobsHaven.com* ran down his sleeve.

Adam took his seat and looked at Alan for the first time. He had ditched the offensive T-shirts for his customary Brioni suit, now all business. Unusually quiet, he actually looked nervous for the first time. Wetness gleamed on his hands and neck. Alan wanted to win, but he needed the money. Thirty-five million dollars would do a lot to ease his troubles, at least for a little while.

The announcers made their prediction, expectations split between them concerning who would be victorious. Then the phrase known around the world erupted through the speakers— "Cards in the air!" The room was electric with excitement.

It was a back and forth from the beginning, two of the best squaring off, each looking for a sliver of opportunity. Soon Alan bet out, representing an ace. Adam raised, and Alan reraised, putting $8 million in the pot. Adam slowed and began analyzing Alan's play in his head, how he bet what the possibilities were—maybe two pairs aces and nines. If he called, it would cost him another $2 million, but at this point the information was worth it. He called with $10 million in the pot going into the river, and the queen of clubs came.

Adam paused after the check, looking down at his chips and then watching Alan's reaction. He couldn't see his eyes through the glasses, but his hands shifted upward. Enough to give Adam the impression the adrenaline had kicked in. Alan wanted him to bet. He pretended to be really thinking about making a bet, going so far as to ask the dealer for a chip count. Then giving the impression of reluctance, he flipped over his pocket eights, revealing his trips. Alan flipped over a six and a seven of clubs, revealing his straight—the winning hand.

At their fifteen-minute break, Adam possessed thirty-five percent of the chips and Alan sixty-five percent. The last hand had tipped the chip count further in Alan's direction. Adam knew he would try to press after the break, to chip away at his stack with aggressive play.

Alan took pictures, signed autographs, and posted comments and pics of the chip stacks on social media. He was back to his old self, taunting Adam and anyone in the crowd who wore a red T-shirt. Adam sat stone still, giving no reaction. Instead he waited, preparing himself for what was to come and praying for continued clarity of thought.

After three warnings to return to the table, Alan finally took his seat. He stared at Adam, making a show of it, trying to intimidate him.

Adam stared back at him, through him, as the cards slid in front of them. He thought maybe he should flip the script, get in Alan's head not through vulgar unprofessional nonsense but irritation and frustration. Not with words but with his play to keep Alan guessing. He was taking a chance, but Alan would never see it coming.

Adam's cards were king of hearts and three of hearts, garbage. He called, and Alan looked down at his hand pocket Queens. Adam called, committed to the bluff, and the flop came: three of spades, ace of hearts, and seven of diamonds. Alan bet $2 million, and Adam reraised to $12 million, leaving Alan to pause, unsure of the bet. He called. Twenty-five million dollars stood in the pot between them. Out came the turn card, nine of hearts, and Adam pushed all in.

Alan now had to make a decision. Adam sat perfectly still, with no expression, as though he was asleep with his eyes open, leaving Alan to play the hand over and over in his mind trying to determine what Adam was holding. The only card he could win with if Adam was holding an ace was a queen, a two outer.

Alan laughed. "Nice ace. You took a real chance with just aces. But I got your number. You can't beat me. You don't have what it takes. No imagination."

Adam said nothing, just did the one thing he had never done in his professional career, for the sole purpose of setting Alan ablaze. He displayed no emotion, just flipped the cards over face up, exposing his king three bluff.

Alan exploded, swearing and talking to the audience. He even stood over Adam screaming obscenities until security intervened. Adam never moved or even looked up at him. Security escorted Alan back to his seat while he continued to make a show of it. Now Adam was the chip leader. He had $35 million in chips and Alan $25 million. Adam chipped away over the next few hands, taking advantage of Alan's frustration and the embarrassment he felt after the bluff. He started getting good cards and was maximizing the opportunity.

Seven hours into the finale, the chip count was Adam's $47 million to Alan's $13 million. Adam didn't let the count cloud his vision. In poker a few good hands could change everything. The stress was getting to Alan. His collar was soaked, and he was sweating so profusely that the smell of cologne and alcohol surrounded him.

Alan pushed all in pre-flop. Adam was holding pocket jacks, he thought heads-up, $13 million to call and the possibility of putting the match to bed. It was the right move, so he called, flipping his cards onto the table. Alan turned over ace, king two over cards, and they both immediately knew Adam had a 53.5% chance of winning. He held the advantage, as small as it was, but knew he made the right call mathematically.

It was now up to the cards, and the crowd and Alan were on their feet. Alan paced, trying to scream Ace-King into existence while Adam sat watching the dealer deliver the flop. The flop came three of clubs, ten of spades, nine of diamonds. Alan had his groupies chant, "Ace-King, Ace-King," and then out came the turn card, a jack, giving Adam trips.

Alan changed the chant to, "Queen, queen, queen," that would give him a straight and his fans followed along.

The dealer took longer to deal the river card, adding to the anticipation. Finally, he peeled the card from the deck, flipping it onto the felt. Five of clubs, making Adam the winner.

The whole auditorium erupted in deafening noise, and security didn't bother trying to stop Lizzy as she ran out to hug Adam. Alan stared in shock at the cards, then stormed off the set, refusing to be interviewed or even shake his opponent's hand.

Adam hugged his wife, then led Lizzy into the stands to celebrate with Caliste, Beth, and Liam. The announcers discussed Adam's shocking show of emotion as he smiled, hugged friends, and shook the hands of those wearing the Jacob's Haven T-shirts. When he was finished, everyone accompanied him as he completed the required post-event interviews.

It was midnight by the time they all returned to Adam's suite for a private dinner. Everyone sat around the table, still chatting and retelling the events of the day. Excitement remained in the air until the adrenaline and caffeine started to wear off. The donations were coming in right up until the last hand.

"Do we have a final number yet on donations during the event?" Adam asked.

Liam checked his phone and his eyes went wide. "The total during the event was $18, 525,317, which puts our total since we launched the site at $32,412,772. That's before your match, though, so give me a second. I need my calculator."

Adam already had the answer. "The match puts the total at $50,938,089, all of it going to fund Jacob's Haven."

Right then, the emotional release of stress that had been the last four days manifested itself in smiles and tears.

Chapter 26

I'll See Ya When I See Ya

They all arrived home in time for Beth and Lizzy to make it to school. Liam convinced Adam to take a day off to rest, then went home to do the same. They needed to have clear heads for the onslaught of decisions they would be making in the weeks to come.

Adam sat on the back porch with Miss Mabel while Clayton and Caliste packed for the trip home. It was hard for him to say goodbye, especially since they had been through so much together. Every time they parted ways, he feared he'd never see her again. "I'll be at the house in a few weeks, scouting out locations for the first Jacob's Haven in New Orleans," he said. "So it won't be long before I see you all again."

Miss Mabel smiled at him. "You know, I prayed coming here would give me peace... that with Jacob and Jack, everything that's happened, you'd be okay. Child, I'm leaving here with my prayers answered, joy in my heart. God's done open your eyes to what he can do, and you all gone be all right now. I was trying to see for you, show you, but now you gots to see for yourself." She nodded. "I'm proud of the man of God you've become, but I'm going to stick around on this earth a while longer just in case you need some reminding. Don't think it's going to be easy, the devil he fittin' to come for you. What you all doing—Jacob's Haven, putting God first, not afraid to share your faith, got people around you following the Word—there's going to be temptations, hard times. You're going to ask some questions. Some things ain't going to make no sense to you, but never forget the good Lord's got your back. If he's first, child, then you know everything else gone be just fine."

Adam looked into her eyes of wisdom. She never ceased to amaze him. "What should I do?" he asked. "How do I protect myself from his attacks?"

Miss Mabel sipped her chicory-infused coffee. "You got to be in the Word. God tells us to put on his armor. You best be buckling up. You gone need all those pieces of armor, cause the devil fittin' to try to mess you up. The Bible says, 'in the beginning was the Word, and the Word was with God, and the Word was God.' You start with that. Get to studying his Word. The Word is the sword of the Spirit that you need to be swingin'. Keep surrounding yourself with church folk who be holdin' you accountable. We all get tested. You need a community holdin' you up."

Clayton came out to let Miss Mabel know they were all packed and ready to go.

Adam walked them to the car, opened the front door, and helped Miss Mabel inside. After hugging Clayton and Caliste, he wished them safe travels and thanked them for everything. He walked to the passenger door and gave the universal wrist motion to lower the window.

Miss Mabel did.

"You know how much I hate saying goodbye," he said. "I'd rather just say something like 'until next time.'"

She grinned and scowled out the front window for a few moments, like she was searching for something in her thoughts. Finally, she looked back to him. "I'll see ya when I see ya."

Adam waived as the car backed up and turned around to leave. He couldn't help laughing at Miss Mabel, her seat pulled as far forward as it would go so she could watch the road as Clayton drove.

Adam strolled down to the pool. He hadn't gone inside the guest house since Jacob's body was removed, and he wanted to make sure nothing was left behind. Soon it would be Paul's, at least for a while.

He opened the door and looked around. Lizzy had replaced all the furniture except for the kitchen table and chairs, which Adam had insisted on keeping. The place also had new paint and different pictures and decorations that gave it a more Scandinavian feel. The table definitely didn't fit in, but Lizzy understood its meaning. He sat down at the table, visualizing Jacob across from him, his Bible opened, a bottle of Gatorade and cup of coffee within reaching distance, and the blanket wrapped around his shoulders.

Adam sat there a moment, sealing the image in his memory, not wanting it to ever fade. After a few minutes, he walked back outside and pulled from his pocket Jacob's envelope addressed to him. Liam received a similar envelope, with their name and instructions on the front that read *Open in one year from the date of my death.*

As much as he wanted to open it, he respected Jacob's wish and put it back in his pocket before sitting in a chair on the little porch by the pool—the place where they had spent so much time together. Adam had soaked in the wisdom and asked Jacob questions, looking for clarity and understanding.

Theo's question about the water and the tree ran through his mind, and he remembered Jacob talking about the fig tree, how Jesus saw Nathaniel under it before Philip called him. He believed Jesus was telling Nathaniel that he could see him in Adam before he was flesh, that he was part of God's plan and he saw him from the beginning. That like Nathaniel, it was the same for all of God's children. The water represented baptism, cleansing or purification, and a statement of his commitment to Christ. Maybe Adam was reaching, and the exhaustion of the past week was catching up to him. Only Jacob knew the answer.

Adam stood and started his walk back to the house. After a few steps, he looked back at the empty chair once occupied by his friend. Not wanting to say goodbye, he instead chose the words that made him smile: "I'll see ya when I see ya."

ACKNOWLEDGMENTS

There's a group of guys that meet once a week for an hour. They are men from all walks of life working to provide encouragement, guidance and support to each other. God is the truth that they all aspire to and the Word a blueprint for action. The time they spend together exists in a safe space free of judgement or ego, where listening, love and faith bring enlightenment. If it was not for the help of these men Harry, Randy, George A., Chris, Attila, Paul, Matt, Dave, George O., Junior, Jim, Fouad (The Whispering Warrior), Terry, Dave A., John, Jay and Jonny, I and many others would still be lost. There are more, too many to list that have come and gone over the years but every one of them impacted me greatly and I am forever grateful.

My wife for her love, support, understanding, forgiveness and unfaltering belief in us. I can't wait to see how the second half plays out when we are both looking up.

My children for teaching me patience, acceptance and tolerance. Thanks for showing me the meaning of unconditional love.

Harry, thanks for taking the long drive with me to Scottsdale. Since that day I've been, "All In", your support and sacrifice helped open my eyes to the truth.

Randy, thanks for the invitation that helped save my life and your faithful friendship.

Al and Char, you never judged but instead supplied unconditional love and support, thank you.

George and Natasha, you've always been there for my family through the peaks and valleys, thank you.

Christ Church of the Valley (C.C.V.) the church I call home to all those that lead, volunteer and support you make a difference in all the lives you touch.

My parents who gave me a love for learning and knowledge, you both taught me so much about a great many things, thank you.

Those I loved and cherished that went on to be with Jesus, I picture you in the stands looking down. I smile knowing that now you have a reason to cheer.

Matt, the one person who knew me before I knew myself. Thank you for your friendship, loyalty and support.

Bryan, "The Bear", after all these years of cherished friendship we both share a love for Jesus and a desire to pass it along to our children.

Don and Bonnie thanks for your wisdom and kindness. You both are a shining light in the darkness.

Jason and Jamie, you've stood by me when it would have been far easier to walk away, thank you.

Galen Bernard, a selfless man of God that made a tremendous impact on the lives he touched.

Junior, for our conversations, your friendship and showing me the true meaning of courage.

The incredible preachers and men of God I've met and listened to along the way. I am forever grateful for your knowledge concerning the things of God.

"From the Outhouse to the Penthouse", and every place in between is a true depiction of my life so far. Those experiences, the people that have supported me through the worst and best of times and God's grace are the reasons I was able to write this book. It is meant to reach the lost, the fence walkers and those that struggle with forgiveness. The greatest gift to give and receive is forgiveness.

For more information, visit

www.TerranceAdam.com

Made in the USA
Monee, IL
31 October 2020

46342491R00146